BABYSITTER OMEGA

GLASS BAY APARTMENTS #3

ARIA GRACE

SURRENDERED PRESS

Surrendered Press

Babysitter Omega

Copyright © 2021 by Aria Grace

All rights reserved.

No part of this book may be reproduced in any form or by any electronic or mechanical means, including information storage and retrieval systems, without written permission from the author, except for the use of brief quotations in a book review.

CONTENTS

1. Luke 1

2. Soren 9

3. Luke 21

4. Soren 35

5. Luke 43

6. Soren 55

7. Luke 67

8. Soren 75

9. Luke 83

10. Soren 93

11. Luke 101

12. Soren 115

13. Luke 127

14. Soren 139

15. Luke 147

16. Soren 155

17. Luke 171

18. Soren 179

19. Luke 189

20. Soren 197

21. Soren 207

22. Soren 221

Epilogue 231

Also by Aria Grace 243

LUKE

Ever feel like you're on top of the world?

Let me know what it's like, because I've never been there.

Kicking a pebble across the nearly empty parking lot, I continue to pace beside my aggravatingly silent car. The old clunker has been threatening to give out for a while now, so I really wasn't surprised when it sputtered to its final resting place on my way to get groceries. I just wish it had waited until I'd made the return trip back to my apartment. The sun is setting, and I'm getting some sketchy vibes from the neighborhood around the store.

I check the time again. When I called for a tow truck, they said it would be about an hour. That estimate came and went about twenty minutes ago. The ice cream sitting in my trunk is probably soup by now.

Frustrated as hell, I look up at the twilit sky and watch the first few stars of the night starting to make their appearance. I'll probably see the moon before the tow truck finally arrives.

Of all the days for this to happen, why did it have to be today?

I work as a babysitter at Omega for Hire, a job-placement agency that helps omegas find work in the city. It's a really useful resource for the omega community in the area.

But you've got to be the right sort of omega if you want clients to hire you in the first place.

And apparently, I'm just not that type of omega because no one seems to want me looking after their kid. Not that I really blame them. I've got a medical condition that makes my schedule pretty damn inconvenient at times. When you're a busy parent looking for a consistent and reliable caretaker, the last thing you want is a nanny who has to take random days off each month.

The one couple that actually did hire me ended my contract today. I guess one of them decided to quit their job and become a stay-at-home parent. Good for them.

Bad for me.

No work. No open contracts. And now, my car is busted, which means no hope of getting it repaired any time soon. If, by some miracle, I do get a new client, I'll have to take the bus or walk to get to work. Not ideal, but I'll make it work. Not that it'll be easy.

I'm not exactly out of shape, but walking isn't my favorite pastime, and I might have an unhealthy relationship with ice cream, which doesn't keep me at my ideal weight.

While taking the bus might save me from the trauma of fresh air and exercise, I absolutely loathe public transportation. Too many people are forced to stand too close together. The last time I was on a bus, some pervert grabbed my ass. While stuff like that probably doesn't happen every day, I definitely don't want to risk it.

Plus, there's my condition.

Frowning, I cross my arms over my chest and force the air out of my lungs. Where is that damn tow truck? When I look in any direction, there are just rundown buildings and groups of rowdy-looking guys.

I need to get out of here.

My cell phone rings in my pocket, startling me back to my present predicament. Probably the tow company updating me on the status of the truck. My money is on having to wait another hour, at least.

The caller ID reads "Farron OFH" and my heart skips a beat. There's only one reason why the omega who runs Omega for Hire would call me.

With my fingers and toes crossed for good luck, I answer the call. "Farron, it's good to hear from you."

"Luke! Thank God you answered." Farron sounds relieved and more flustered than I've ever heard him. "How are you doing?"

I glance down at my silent car and shake my head. "I'm just dandy." I hope he can hear my cheery smile through the phone because I can't pretend any harder. "What can I do for you?"

"Would you be interested in a babysitting contract? It's a last-minute thing." The sound of rustling papers crinkles in the phone. "The client is a single dad, alpha, who needs someone to watch his kid while he's at work during the week."

I take a moment to swallow my excitement and try to remain professional. Meanwhile, my brain is screaming at me to just take the job and not ask too many questions. "How long is the contract for?"

"Indefinite," Farron says. "It's an open-ended contract."

And there goes my bubble of excitement. "So, the client can end it whenever he wants." I've been down this road before, and it's never good.

"I know it's not ideal. No one else was interested in it either. But I thought maybe you'd be willing to give it a shot?" Farron doesn't have to say what he's really thinking. It's clear as day. He knows I'm not in a position to refuse.

I was nobody's first choice for this job, but I'm the only one who can't say no to any amount of employment, as temporary as it may be.

To be perfectly honest, Farron is a great guy. He gave me a shot despite my medical issues and has gone to bat for me several times when it came to landing contracts. And I totally understand that at the end of the day, he is running a business.

I take a deep breath and wait for this whole opportunity to fall apart with my next question. "Does he know about my conditions for the contract?"

It's Farron's turn to be quiet for a moment. I'm sure I hear the sound of him tapping his fingers against the desk as he considers his next words. "I wanted to make sure you were willing to take the job before I reached out to him again. But I've got a good sense about this whole thing. The client is desperate for a babysitter because he's got zero experience with kids. You've got great references and a good work history. Your conditions shouldn't even be a factor."

They shouldn't, but they usually are.

People always get spooked when they hear about my days off. What if the timing interferes with something important? What if I need a day off at a really inconvenient time? It's a whole thing.

"Do I have your permission to extend a contract to the client?" Farron prods.

I don't want to get my hopes up. I really don't. I can't even count the number of times Farron has submitted my contract to clients and they've come back with a polite refusal. It's crushing.

The tow truck finally arrives in the parking lot and slowly approaches my lifeless vehicle.

If I want any chance of fixing my car, let alone paying my rent, I'll have to put myself out there and try to land a new client. I can't let my fear of rejection get in the way of my only chance at a paycheck.

"Fine," I say as I lift my free hand to wave down the tow truck. "Send him my contract. Just shoot me a text when you get his answer."

"Yeah, will do." Farron's enthusiastic response gives me the tiniest bit of hope. He seems confident about the opportunity, so maybe I'll be pleasantly surprised when he gets back to me.

When the line goes silent, I pocket my phone and try to steady my nerves.

It's hard not to get excited about the possibility of a long-term job. I love kids and have so much fun working with them. I wanted to be a teacher when I was younger, but college wasn't exactly in the cards for a poor omega from the wrong side of town. Babysitting is the next best thing as far as I'm concerned.

But every contract ends the same way.

"I'm sorry, you're lovely, but it just won't work." They all say the same crap as they smile and show me to the door. In fact, I've collected an impressive list of glowing references this way. I just need to find someone who's actually willing to meet me halfway on this.

Once I do that, maybe I'll finally find out what it's like to be on top of the world.

2
____

SOREN

I LOOK over the contract for the hundredth time. "You've got to be kidding me."

The omega on the other side of the desk folds his hands over his closed laptop and just looks at me.

"He needs a few random days off every month because of some medical condition?" Is it me or am I being taken advantage of here? Either way, I'm desperate, and this Farron guy knows it.

Omega for Hire is highly recommended, and Farron's got a reputation of providing high-quality omegas to do whatever job you need, so I'll sign whatever contract he puts in front of me. Even if this seems unreasonable.

"It's a maximum of three consecutive days each month," Farron says, leaning back in his chair with a knowing smile. "Luke is definitely worth the inconvenience. He's very good at what he does. There's no better omega to look after your little one. And, he just had a cancellation, so he's free. It's fate!"

Frowning, I raise an eyebrow at his enthusiasm, unable to go so far as to call it "fate." But the list of references Farron provided for me do seem to be legit.

The clock on the wall above the desk is making my blood pressure go up. I have to get back home soon. My current emergency babysitter can't hang around much longer. "Fine, I'll sign the contract. It's open-ended, right? I can cancel without penalty?"

"Yes, absolutely." Farron grabs a pen off the desk and hands it to me. "If you'd like, I can call you when another babysitter becomes available. Then you'll have the option to start a new contract if you're unhappy with Luke's performance."

"That sounds fine." I quickly scrawl my name on the dotted line, anxious to get out of here and back home.

"I'm certain you'll be quite happy with Luke's service, though." Farron speaks confidently as he takes the contract and gives it a once-over. "I don't mean to brag, but I'm pretty good at matching clients with the perfect omega to suit their needs."

"That's what I'm hoping." I rise from my seat and slip my hands into my pockets. "He's able to start tomorrow?"

"Yes," Farron confirms with a nod. "He'll be there bright and early, as requested."

I smooth the wrinkles from my shirt and glance around the plush interior of the office. "Okay, then...I guess I'll be heading out."

"Thank you again for choosing Omega for Hire," Farron calls after me as I slip through the glass door of the office and out into the hallway.

My new car is waiting for me in the parking lot. It's pure white with tinted windows. The sort of car that oozes status. At least, that's what I thought when I bought it. But now, it's surrounded by half a dozen cars that probably cost two or three times more than mine did. Omega for Hire has a good reputation among the upper class, but I didn't realize it was this good.

After slipping into my vehicle, I quickly head back toward home. I've got a long way to go and traffic sucks. I'll have to find a way to make this up to Arlo somehow.

Slowly, the crowded city streets start to thin out and traffic becomes lighter. The tension in my shoulders releases when I hit the edge of the city and find myself just a short walk from the beach.

This is where I love to be.

Glass Bay Apartments greet me like an old friend. I was one of the first tenants to move in when they opened their doors, and it was easily one of the best decisions I've ever made. Quiet neighborhood, great neighbors, nice apartments, and the rent is reasonable. Sure, I've added a few more minutes to my daily commute, but I don't mind the extra drive time.

Normally, I wouldn't hesitate to head straight up to my apartment. It's my personal haven. My refuge from the stresses of the world.

At least, it used to be.

Now, I park the car and rest my hands on the steering wheel as the engine slowly cools. I'm already late, another minute to collect my thoughts and prepare myself won't hurt anything. I've had to make a lot of adjustments over the last few days, and I'd like to think I'm handling it pretty well, all things considered.

Of course, hiding in my car isn't exactly "handling" things.

Which means it's time to face reality.

My apartment is located on the first floor of the farthest building. Across the lawn of the U-shaped courtyard, just a few doors down from the owners.

As I walk across the lawn, a few of my neighbors are out and about. They wave their hellos and one or two call out to me. In addition to everything else, moving to Glass Bay Apartments has been great for my social life. I'd hoped I'd hit it off with one of the cute omegas living here, since it's hard to date when you have a demanding job. But so far, I haven't had much luck.

When I reach my door, I take a deep breath and walk inside, prepared for anything that may be waiting for me.

"There you are!" Arlo cheers from the sofa where he's playing a video game with a kid who's about five years old.

My kid.

The kid doesn't look up at me. He keeps his gaze fixed on the TV where he's expertly navigating the video game they've been playing.

"Sorry I'm late." I try to smile apologetically. "I got caught in traffic."

"Don't worry about it." Arlo rises from the sofa and stretches. "Not like I've got plans. Other than hanging out with the girls."

Arlo collectively refers to his three cats as "the girls." For the longest time, I thought he was in some sort of harem relationship or something. Turns out, he's just a single omega who plays a few too many video games and talks to his cats.

"Do you want to stay for dinner?" I offer as I make my way toward the refrigerator. "I don't mind setting another plate."

"No, no, don't bother." Arlo waves his hands in protest. "I need to give the girls their dinner soon. Plus, I've got a looming deadline I really should work on." He glances toward the nearby wall clock with a bit of a disgusted look on his face.

"I'm really sorry I ran so late." Arlo's one of the few friends I've made since moving in, and I hate taking advantage of our friendship. "If there's any way I can make up for it, I'll be glad to."

"You don't owe me anything." Arlo shoots me a friendly wink as he saunters across the room and reaches for the front door. "You're not the reason I'm behind schedule. That's all my own fault." He pauses as he looks back toward the sofa. "Adrien, you should show your dad that thing you showed me. The hidden passage you found, remember?"

Adrien, the kid...my kid...looks up from his game and frowns at Arlo. He then slowly turns toward me. His big green eyes look so much like mine. I have to admit, at first I didn't believe my ex when he showed up and told me I had a kid.

Now, I can't deny it.

Especially because the DNA test sitting in my office leaves no room for debate.

"Are you coming back?" Adrien asks, shifting his gaze back to Arlo.

"Maybe tomorrow." Arlo's eyes are kind as he tries to silently reassure Adrien that I'm not the enemy. "I gotta go back to my house for now, though."

Adrien looks at me uncertainly. He hasn't exactly been receptive to the whole situation, but that's to be expected. Being dropped off with a strange alpha is as big of a change for him as it is for me.

Without another word, Adrien turns his attention back to his game.

Arlo offers me an apologetic smile and shrugs. "I'll stop by tomorrow after I get this project finished. It probably won't be until later in the day, though."

"We'll be fine," I assure him. "Thanks for everything. You've been a lifesaver."

"I'll expect you to return the favor someday." Arlo winks and then laughs when he sees my puzzled expression. "I'm going to a conference next month.

Maybe you and Adrien can feed the girls and check in on them while I'm gone?"

"Oh, yeah, of course. I don't mind looking after them for you." I've never really been much of an animal person, but cats are okay. They mostly do their own thing, which is fine with me.

"Perfect!" Arlo yanks open the front door with a flourish. "I'll see you guys tomorrow!"

Without Arlo's boisterous energy to flood the room, I'm left with the awkward tension that's existed since my ex stopped by three days ago.

Adrien doesn't even look at me as I stand there staring at him in exasperation.

But I'm the adult here. The parent. So I have to learn how to deal with things on my own. With a deep breath, I force myself into the kitchen to put together some sort of meal. I used to pride myself on how much home cooking I did. I've developed a somewhat refined palate thanks to all my experiments I've perfected over the years.

Only the best ingredients graced the shelves of my kitchen a few days ago.

Since Adrien's arrival, I've had to completely reframe my thinking. Apparently, kids prefer things like fish sticks and chicken nuggets. At least, those are the only things I've been able to get him to eat.

I chuck some chicken nuggets in the oven and try to work some of the kinks out of my neck. It feels like I haven't had a chance to breathe properly in days. There are times when I look around and have no idea who I am or how I got here. It's funny how something as simple as finding out you've got a kid can completely up-end your entire existence.

Hopefully, this babysitter will give me a chance to figure out my life a little bit. Even with the weird stipulation in his contract, I'll have more time to myself than I do now. And I'll be able to actually put in an appearance at work instead of telecommuting full-time like I've done for these last few days. Getting back into some sort of schedule will be nice.

But as far as my relationship with Adrien goes...

I look over at him as he prods at the buttons on his controller. I don't know what to make of him, really. I've never been good with kids and definitely never pictured myself as a dad. But it's not like I was going to turn him away. I feel responsible for him. Like I owe it to him to try to make up for all the time I've missed out on.

I just don't have the slightest idea about how to do that.

3

———

LUKE

Bright and early is not my forte. Especially not when the buses don't start running for another hour. Hiring a ride share at this godforsaken hour is crazy expensive, but it's the only option I've got to make it all the way across town in time.

Thankfully, I received an advance on the contract, so maybe I'll be able to get someone to look at my car soon. I just hope it's not going to cost too much.

After I thank my driver, I stumble out of the vehicle and onto the nearby sidewalk. The sign for Glass Bay Apartments marks the driveway to the parking lot.

I'm pleasantly surprised by how nice the place looks. I remember what this place looked like just a few years ago. The apartments had been affordable, but the buildings appeared to be on the verge of collapse.

The new owners have really cleaned the place up.

Glancing at the hastily scrawled note on the back of my hand, I memorize the apartment number. The buildings are laid out in a pretty logical way, so it's not hard to find my way around.

In just a few short minutes, I'm knocking on the front door of my new employer. There's a familiar boulder of anticipation in my stomach, and I'm a bundle of nerves, half expecting to be told I'm no longer needed as soon as the door opens. That's just the sort of week I've been having.

My new boss swings open the front door and gives me a quick once-over. "You must be Luke."

I stand in dumb silence as I check him out. He looks like he walked right off the pages of a menswear catalog. Not a hair is out of place, and he has a smile that makes my toes curl as I try not to drool all over him. His gorgeous green eyes pierce through me and make me feel like he can see every thought in my head.

"Umm...ummm...yeah, yes. That's me." I finally remember my manners and hold out a hand. "I'm the babysitter you hired."

"Great. I'm Soren." He shakes my hand then steps back and gestures for me to walk inside. "Adrien's still in bed. I've mostly just been letting him get up when he feels like it."

I purse my lips as I glance around the interior of the apartment. It's very posh, and all the furniture is expensive and...planned? I don't think that's the right word to describe how it feels, but that's the best I can come up with. The whole apartment looks designed and doesn't really feel like a home, much less a place where a kid lives.

At least, not a happy kid.

"Please, make yourself at home." Soren moves toward the kitchen where a coffee pot percolates on the counter. "Coffee?"

"No, I'm fine, thanks." I peel off my coat and slowly begin circling the living room. There's no personal touches to the room. No family pictures or awards or anything I'd expect to find.

"I'm glad you were able to make it over here so early." Soren pours himself a cup and leans on the counter to face me. "I'm afraid my work demands early hours."

"That's fine," I assure him. "I don't mind early mornings. I'll be here when you need me."

I can sense him looking at me quizzically, but I don't make eye contact. I can't let myself worry about what he's thinking right now. I've got to prepare myself for what's to come.

Normally, I can get a good idea about a family and the kids I'll be caring for just by walking through the house. But this place feels incredibly disjointed. It's a bachelor pad, really. The bachelor pad of an alpha with a really good career and lots of upward mobility. The kind of guy who hasn't even considered settling down yet. He cares about his appearance and his surroundings, but isn't so vain as to plaster the walls with his face and his achievements.

This is not a home where a child has lived.

"Can I ask you something?" I finally enter the kitchen and lean against the counter opposite of where Soren is finishing up his coffee.

"I guess." He seems somewhat guarded as he looks at me. I'm sure he's got all kinds of questions of his own to ask.

"Well..." I take a deep breath as I try to figure out how to say this in the most diplomatic way possible. "Exactly how long has Adrien lived with you?"

Soren lowers his coffee cup to the counter and lets his shoulders relax slightly. "I guess it's obvious that I'm not used to the whole 'dad' thing."

I lift a brow and watch him as he adjusts the buttons on his shirtsleeves.

"Five years ago, I was in a serious relationship with Adrien's other dad. I ended things with him when I found out he was cheating on me. I haven't even thought about him since." Soren exhales forcefully and looks over at me. "Three days ago, my ex showed up on my doorstep with Adrien in tow. He said 'here's your kid if you want him. I'm heading to LA. Don't bother looking for me.'"

"You can't be serious." My brow creases, and I fold my arms over my chest in disbelief.

"I have no reason to lie." Soren shrugs and tilts his head slightly as he looks at me. "As far as I can tell, things haven't really been going well for my ex. He didn't look great. But he somehow managed to track me down and brought Adrien here. He didn't really give me a choice in the matter either. Not that I was going to turn away my own kid."

I bite my lip to keep from asking the obvious question.

"And yes, he's mine." Soren doesn't miss a beat. "I've already confirmed it. Though, even if he wasn't...it's not like I'm going to kick a kid out in the street. He hasn't done anything wrong but his whole life has been upended because of his idiot father. Everything he knows has changed, and he was left with a complete stranger that he has no connection to and who has absolutely no idea how to be a proper parent." Soren clears his throat and straightens his shoulders. "My point is, I know I'm not cut out for this. That's why I hired you."

I open my mouth to try to explain that I'm just a babysitter. I'm not trained in healing deep emotional trauma or abandonment issues. But before I can say anything, I see movement out of the corner of my eye.

A little boy with bright blond hair shuffles into the living room, climbs onto the sofa, and picks up the video game controller on the coffee table. A moment later, the TV glows with life and the sounds of a video game drift into the kitchen.

I frown and look back at Soren.

"That's all he does," he explains with a helpless shrug. "He won't talk to me. I can barely get him to eat anything other than frozen, breaded, junk food."

My heart tightens as I look back at Adrien. I don't know if I'm the right person to help him, but I've got to at least try.

"I wish I had more time with you, but I've got to get to the office before my boss has a fit. My neighbor, Arlo, said he might stop in later. Adrien seems to like him. He talks to him at least."

I nod slowly as the broad-shouldered alpha gathers up his briefcase and car keys from the kitchen table.

He charges toward the front door but hesitates a moment before leaving. He looks back at Adrien, as if he's trying to make up his mind about something. "I'm heading to work now, Adrien. Luke is going to look after you while I'm gone, okay?"

Adrien doesn't look at him or me.

Soren's beautiful green eyes look sad, but he forces a smile when he turns back to me. "My contact information is on the counter. If you need anything, send me a text and I'll get back to you when I can. If it's an emergency, call and I'll answer right away but—"

"Only if it's an emergency," I finish for him. "Don't worry, I know the drill."

Soren nods. "Right, of course. Okay. I'll be back around seven." A moment later, he's gone.

As soon as the door closes, Adrien looks over at me. "Are you supposed to be my other dad too?"

Uh...what? "No, I'm just here to look after you." I head into the living room to try to get him to open up.

"I don't need anyone to look after me." Adrien turns back at his game. "My dad said I was big enough to look after myself."

I purse my lips before replying. He must be talking about Soren's ex. "Sure, but looking after yourself is kinda lonely. Isn't it?"

Adrien's mouth curls into a frown. He looks sad as he slowly nods. "Yeah, I guess."

"That's why I'm here." I keep my voice upbeat. "So you don't have to be alone."

"I guess that's okay." Adrien peeks over at me after a moment. "Are you going to play video games with me? Arlo played with me yesterday. That was fun."

Kids on screens all day is a bit of a pet peeve of mine. "How about this? I'll play games with you for a little while, but you need to do a few things first."

"Like what?" Adrien narrows his eyes at me suspiciously.

"Well, let's start with getting dressed and brushing your teeth. Then maybe we'll have some breakfast?" It's clear that he's been left to his own devices for the last few days. I doubt anyone's been forcing him to keep up on his hygiene, and it probably hasn't even crossed Soren's mind to try.

Adrien seems smug as he climbs off the sofa. "I don't have a toothbrush."

Well, that's an issue. I hide my frown and change gears. "Okay, well, put on some clean clothes and we'll get some breakfast. Then we'll figure out the toothbrush thing later."

"And you'll play with me?"

"Yeah, we'll play for a little while. And we'll go to the park for a bit. I saw a really cool playground nearby." I offer him a wide smile.

Adrien doesn't look thrilled with the idea, but he doesn't fight me. "Okay."

"So, why don't you show me your bedroom?" I gesture toward the hallway.

Adrien nods and marches down the hall. "It's not really my bedroom. My bedroom is with my dad," he explains as he pushes the door open to what looks like a guest room in a hotel.

It's definitely not a child's room, that's for sure. There's a step stool next to the queen-sized bed, and other than a small stuffed bear by the pillows, the room is pretty much devoid of stuff for a kid.

"This bed's a bit too big for you, huh?" I start straightening out the blankets and tucking everything in properly.

"It's not bad." Adrien drags a small backpack out from under the bed and starts digging through it. "I miss my real bed, though."

I sit down on the floor beside him as he dumps his backpack out on the floor.

"Did your dad tell you anything about why he brought you here?" I don't want to open up any sore spots with the kid, but it's clear that Adrien hasn't accepted that this is supposed to be his new home.

"He said he got a new job but he had to move away and I couldn't come." Adrien doesn't look up while he's talking. "So told me I was going to go meet my other dad and stay with him."

Damn, this guy was quite the parent. "Is that all he said?"

"He told me to be good." Adrien finally looks up at me with tears in his eyes. "I miss my dad. Why couldn't he take me with him? Why do I have to stay here?"

"Oh, sweetie..." On instinct, I hold out my arms and offer him a hug.

Adrien hesitates for a second but then crawls into my lap and buries his face against my chest as he starts to cry.

Obviously, I don't have the whole story, but from what I've managed to piece together, I don't think Adrien has had a very positive experience with most of the adults in his life.

"Everyone always leaves," he says, sniffling into my shirt. "I'm always alone, and I hate it."

"You're not alone right now," I remind him.

"Are you gonna leave?"

"I'll go home tonight after Soren comes home, but then I'll be here again tomorrow."

Adrien frowns and looks away. "I don't like that guy."

"Who? Soren?"

He nods.

My hackles go up, although I didn't get any bad vibes from the guy. In fact, I got some pretty good ones. "Why not?"

"He tried to make me eat mushrooms." Adrien's nose is wrinkled in disgust. "I hate mushrooms."

"Yikes, I guess I'd hate that too." I give him a solemn nod of solidarity. "But...is that the only reason?"

"He's...he's not my dad."

4

SOREN

As I step out of my morning meeting, I'm feeling pretty good. I didn't miss much in the few days I was gone, so I'm not behind on anything. My coworkers filter past me as they return to their desks and offices as if they didn't even notice I was gone.

Slowly but surely, the sounds of daily office life fill the main room.

This is what I enjoy most about coming to work every day. Everyone here knows what they need to do. Everything is in the right place. There's order, there's a schedule, and I know what to expect from minute to minute.

"Soren, glad you're back." My boss, Robert, claps me on the shoulder. "And good work putting the final touches on the Goldson file while you were away. It was exactly what we needed. I was able to use your work to secure the account and without having to renegotiate any terms of the contract."

"That's great to hear." I put way too much time and effort into that file for it not to pay off in the end. I wasn't about to let it all go up in flames just because I had to work from home for a few days.

"It's better than great," Robert says with a grin. "I'm going to treat you to lunch today." He steps back and waves a pair of finger guns at me as he backpedals toward his office. "You and I have a lot to discuss."

"Looking forward to it." I smile and force myself to maintain a modicum of professionalism. Inside, I'm beyond ecstatic. Lunch with the boss isn't just some casual thing that everyone gets to do.

This is big. Huge, even.

"Twelve-thirty," Robert says, shoving his shoulder against his office door. "I'll meet you by the front door."

"I'll be there." I nod eagerly as he disappears into his office.

It takes all my self-control to walk to my office instead of skipping down the hall while kicking my heels. As soon as my door is closed, I allow myself a silent fist pump in celebration. It's been months, but I'm finally moving up again. There's no way he doesn't want to discuss a promotion. Maybe even partnership.

After a few calming breaths, I compose myself and return to my desk. I've got a lot of work to get done before my lunch date. There's no way I'm going to show up to a promotion discussion with a full inbox and a stack of messages waiting for my attention.

But first...

I fish my phone out of my pocket and quickly check the messages. I'm always getting texts from coworkers who need updates on different projects, so I'm not surprised to see half a dozen messages waiting for me. There's only one that demands my immediate attention, though.

It's from an unknown number, sent over two hours ago, just a few minutes after I entered the meeting.

This is Luke. Just a quick update. I've been going through Adrien's things. He doesn't have a toothbrush or any clean underwear. He actually only has two t-shirts, two pairs of jeans, no socks, and the PJs he was wearing this morning. I'm washing his clothes now, but he'll need a larger wardrobe. Kids go through clothes so fast!

I swear under my breath. I should've known to check Adrien's backpack when he arrived. And what the hell kind of father doesn't even think to make him brush his teeth? Not that he would've listened to me, but I still should have asked about it.

I type out a response to his text after adding Luke to my contacts. *I'll send you some money to go shopping, if you don't mind. Otherwise, it'll have to wait until I get off work.* I pause for a moment, trying to decide if there's anything else I should say. Even I have to admit that the text sounds a little bit cold and stand-offish the way it's worded now. *Is there anything else he needs? I know my place isn't exactly kid friendly.*

I re-read it a few times before finally hitting send. I can't spend too much time overthinking this right now. I want to get my plate cleared before heading to lunch with Robert, and I won't get to everything if I sit here dawdling.

Unfortunately, Luke's reply comes a little more quickly than expected. *There's a lot, actually. I won't get into all the details now, but Adrien and I had a bit of a heart-to-heart this morning. I think he might open up a bit more if he feels more at home here. Making his room feel like it's actually his would probably be a good place to start.*

He won't even talk to me, but he'll have a deep conversation with someone he just met? I rub my temples in frustration. I don't know what I'm doing wrong. He opened up to Arlo too. Maybe it's just me. Maybe he still hasn't forgiven me for the mushrooms.

That seems a bit extreme, though, even for a kid.

I shake my head as I try to refocus myself. There's nothing I can do about any of this now.

I'll send a few hundred. Let me know if you need more. I quickly send the message and switch over to the money-sending app.

As per the contract I signed with Farron, if Luke needs anything to provide for Adrien, it's easy to send him money using the app. The money is then fed directly into an account that's provided to Luke by Omega for Hire so he can care for Adrien. Plus, I don't have to worry about him running off with all the money I just sent him. If anything inappropriate with the money happens—Farron swore up and down that it wouldn't—then Omega for Hire can lock the account and return my money to me.

Luke's next reply is almost instant. *Sure, that's fine. But when you get off work tonight, I'd like to take some time to discuss a few things with you.*

That sounds a bit ominous. Is everything okay? I don't even bother putting my phone down this time. I'm sure I'll get Luke's reply in a few seconds.

More or less. Even over the text, I can sense Luke's unease. Funny, given that I barely know him. *Adrien's been through a lot. I want to make sure that you and I are on the same page. That's all.*

I don't fully understand what he's trying to say, but I guess a full explanation will have to wait until tonight. *Okay, we'll talk tonight.*

Thank you, Luke replies. **Adrien and I will head to the store soon.**

I hesitate before putting the phone down. Is the conversation over? Can I safely go back to work, or is this the sort of situation where I'm supposed to say something else?

After a few seconds of internal debating, I put the phone away and try to get back to work. But it's hard to focus now that I've got a million different questions running through my head. Plus, I can't stop kicking myself for not looking into what Adrien actually had in his backpack.

I just assumed he had everything he needed.

Which was stupid. I should've known better. The sort of man who just dumps their kid off on a guy they haven't seen in five years isn't exactly responsible.

By the time I manage to get back into the groove, I've lost almost an hour of the day. It's going to be hard to make up for it now, but I can't afford to worry about Adrien all day. I mean, that's why I hired Luke.

So I can focus on my job during the day. No matter what.

5

———

LUKE

"So, what do you think?" Adrien is helping me smooth out the wrinkles from his new bedspread. It's bright and cheery, with a colorful graphic of the main character from his favorite video game. He picked it out himself.

"I like it." He climbs up onto the bed. "It's the one I always wanted."

"It's perfect, then." I offer him a meaningful smile.

He seems a bit more animated now than he was this morning. A couple hours of running around at the playground boosted his mood quite a bit. Then we went shopping, and he got to pick out a bunch of awesome stuff. We didn't even spend all the money Soren sent us, so we stopped for lunch too.

As soon as we got home, we set up all the bedroom stuff he picked out. Curtains, a lamp for the nightstand, the bedspread, and a few other random items. It's a bit mismatched, but at least it looks like a kid lives here now.

We also addressed his clothing situation. He still doesn't have enough clothes to call it a wardrobe, but at least he can change his socks and underwear every day.

Adrien arranges his teddy bear on the bed by his pillows and stifles a yawn. He's been rubbing at his eyes for a while too, so I'm pretty sure he needs a nap but is trying to hide it.

"We've had a pretty busy day so far." I sigh and sit on the edge of his bed. "A nap doesn't sound like a bad idea."

He frowns at me and looks over at his bear. "I don't take naps. Naps are for babies."

"Naps are awesome," I protest. "Grownups love naps, but no one ever lets us take one."

"Naps mean you can't play."

"But when you're tired, you don't really feel like playing, do you?"

He takes a deep breath, clearly turning everything over in his head. He's very smart for a kid his age and possesses a maturity that most kids don't develop until they're a lot older. It's a little troubling, to be honest. I'm not used to seeing five-year-olds who actually take the time to think about stuff before making decisions.

"I guess I can take a nap." He finally gives in, conditionally. "But not a long one."

"Yeah, of course. Just long enough so you're not tired anymore."

He nods as he kicks off his shoes.

I pull back the blankets and help him slide in. "Do you need anything else?"

Adrien shakes his head slowly and lets out a big yawn.

"Okay, I'll be in the other room if you need me." I walk toward the door, and when I get to it, I glance back at the bed. To my surprise, Adrien is hunkered down beneath the covers, looking at me with fear in his eyes. "What's the matter?" I tilt my head slightly. "Are you okay?"

His voice quivers as he speaks. "Y-yeah…"

I turn back around, giving him my full attention. "If you need anything at all, just ask me. It's okay."

"Are you sure?" He sits up slowly. "You won't get mad?"

"I promise. I won't get mad." I refrain from asking him why the hell I'd be mad at him for asking a simple question, but my hate for Soren's ex is growing by the minute.

"I…I don't like the dark…" Adrien whispers.

"That's okay. Lots of people don't like the dark. I don't like it either. It's not nice when you can't see anything." I smile at him gently to let him know I'm not mad.

"Yeah?" Adrien looks at me, confused. "My dad said only babies are scared of the dark."

"Well, he probably didn't know anyone like me then." I laugh lightly, trying to alleviate some of the tension in the room. I might not be the best equipped for helping kids with emotional baggage, but I know enough not to say anything against their parent. Especially because, despite all the crap, Adrien still seems so attached to the man who dumped him off with a stranger.

"I've got an idea." I hold up my finger then lean out into the hallway, then flip the switch in the hallway. "There's a light here, so if I leave the door open and turn off the big light in here..." As I turn off the overhead light, I notice Adrien flinch at the sound. "It's not so dark now, is it?"

He looks around the room, his expression slowly relaxing as he takes in his surroundings. "I can still see everything."

"Perfect. The big light won't keep you from sleeping, but the light out here will let you see everything." I return to his side and perch on the edge of the bed. "Tomorrow, I'll see about getting you a proper nightlight."

"What's that?" He flops back against his pillows with a much calmer expression on his face.

"It's just a little light that makes things not so dark," I explain. "So you can see at nighttime."

He yawns again. "Okay."

"Ready for your nap?" I pull the blankets up around him nice and snug.

"Yeah..." His eyes drift shut and his clasped hands slip under his cheek. "Goodnight, Luke."

DIGGING THROUGH SOMEONE ELSE'S KITCHEN IS always an interesting experience. No one organizes anything exactly the same way. Things are rarely ever in the places I expect them to be, so it takes me a good ten minutes of opening every single drawer and cupboard before I find exactly what I'm looking for.

I should've taken stock of Soren's kitchen before heading to the store earlier. All he has is a bunch of really fancy ingredients that I can't even pronounce. The sort of stuff that makes my bank account scream just looking at it. I can't help but wonder what his monthly food budget is like.

But now that it's nearly dinner time, I need to come up with something to feed Adrien that isn't fish sticks or chicken nuggets. The kid needs some variety in his diet. Not to mention some damn vegetables.

I glance sidelong toward the living room where Adrien is playing a video game. He seemed to have a good nap and woke up looking refreshed and happy. We went for a walk around the apartment complex to get some fresh air and saw four squirrels along the way. When we found the pool and clubhouse, Adrien made me promise we'd go look around some more tomorrow.

He seemed especially excited by the pool. Maybe I'll bring up swimming lessons to Soren. They usually have classes for kids his age at the community pool downtown, and I'm sure he'd enjoy it.

Refocusing on the kitchen, I manage to find all the ingredients for spaghetti. I'll have to make the sauce from scratch, but I'm pretty confident in my skills. Soren's ingredients might be super expensive, but they'll do the same job my cheap stuff at home does.

Even though it's not really in my contract to make dinner for Soren, it's not like I'm going to do all this work and only make enough food for Adrien to eat alone. Besides, spaghetti is one of those meals that really goes a long way.

Hopefully, he appreciates the effort.

Of course, I'm still a little bit nervous about losing the contract altogether. Doubly so now that I've gotten to know Adrien. With every minute that ticks by, I get a little more anxious that Soren will get home and tell me not to come back tomorrow.

Because that's what happens when people find a replacement babysitter who doesn't have the weird, random clause in their contract that lets them disappear for a few days each month.

I'm not under any delusions here.

I know Soren probably asked Farron to let him know if anyone else becomes available. It's what everyone always does. And eventually, someone else does become available and I'm out the door. I'm the "filler" babysitter. The one you get when no one else can fit you in their schedule.

Because no one wants to deal with someone who doesn't fit cleanly into their lives.

With a deep breath, I try to force all the negativity out of my head. I can't risk that shit coloring my interactions with Adrien at all. The poor kid doesn't deserve it.

So I focus fully on making the best spaghetti I've ever made.

When the whole thing is nearly done, Adrien peeks into the kitchen. From the look on his face, it's clear he's been drawn in by the smell. "What's that?"

"Spaghetti. Do you like spaghetti?" I realize I didn't even bother to ask about his likes. I just assumed spaghetti would be safe since most kids like pasta of all kinds.

"I don't know..." He frowns. "Are we out of fish sticks?"

"No, but I thought we'd try something different tonight. Spaghetti is really good. It's one of my favorites." It's always difficult to get kids to try new foods. They develop extreme opinions about food really easily, especially when they aren't exposed to a variety of flavors.

They either love something or they hate it, and one bad experience can sour them against an entire food group for a really long time.

"Is there mushrooms?" He looks up at the counter suspiciously. "I hate mushrooms."

"There are no mushrooms, I promise." It's a good thing I couldn't find any mushrooms because normally I'd add a handful to the sauce without even thinking.

His cheeks puff out as he exhales dramatically. "I guess I'll try it then."

That's one battle won. I expected to resort to bargaining screen time to get him to eat. Even though the "experts" out there will tell you not to bribe kids into doing things, sometimes that's the only thing that works. As long as you don't rely on it for everything, once in a while doesn't hurt.

Especially if you've got the kid's respect.

A few minutes later, we're settled in at the table with our plates of spaghetti. I opted not to bother with the vegetables tonight. Partially because Soren has absolutely zero "kid-friendly" veggies, and partially because I'm sure Adrien's vegetable experience has been limited. I don't want to introduce too many new things at once.

Especially if he decides he hates spaghetti.

6

———

SOREN

I'M on cloud nine as I stride across the parking lot toward the apartment.

Robert offered me a massive promotion with a significant pay raise. If I accept, I'll be in a position with a lot more responsibility but also a lot more room for advancement. But I haven't gotten this far in life by leaping into things without considering every angle first. It wasn't easy but I kept my excitement muted so I could play the whole thing as casually as possible.

I know Robert was hoping I'd take the promotion on the spot, but I've got something I've got to do first.

This sort of promotion is a powerful tool. The kind of opportunity I can use to get a job at another company with better benefits, a larger salary, better hours, and really, whatever the hell I want out of life. I've just got to be smart about how I approach the negotiation. And I can't sit too long on the offer because these sorts of things have an expiration date on them.

Robert wants my answer by the end of next week. That's a reasonable amount of time to assess the job, look at the market, and make a decision.

As far as my career is concerned, things couldn't possibly be better.

But as I approach my apartment, my steps start to slow. For a second, I forgot about what I'm about to walk into. Mentally, I've got to prepare myself for what's waiting inside.

Normally, I'd come home, kick off my shoes, grab a beer, and watch some TV before taking a shower and heading to bed. If there's a big project I need to work on, I might get out my laptop and try to hammer some of that out too.

But now...everything's different.

I gingerly open the front door, and I'm greeted with the lingering smell of spices. Someone's been cooking something other than frozen junk food.

That's a positive sign.

I was expecting to see Adrien on the sofa where I left him, but he's not there. There's no immediate sign of Luke either. "Um...hello? I'm back." I feel kinda weird calling out like that. It's like that stereotypical "Honey, I'm home!" from all those old TV shows.

"We're in here," Luke calls from the guest bedroom. Actually, I guess it's Adrien's room now.

I set my briefcase and jacket on the kitchen table and cautiously make my way to the bedroom. My heart's pounding for some odd reason. I don't know what I'll find, and I guess that's enough to make my adrenaline spike.

"Hey, what's going on back here?" I smile, trying for the friendliest tone I can manage as I peek into the bedroom.

Luke and Adrien are sitting on the bed with a great big story book.

The room itself has been transformed from the carefully manicured, clean and modern guest bedroom into a rainbow of bright colors and graphic prints. Almost none of the new additions look like they came from the same set. It irks my personal sense of style to no end but...it really does look like a kid's room now.

Adrien no longer looks out of place as he sits on that oversized bed. Though, I should probably look into getting one that's more his size.

"We were just reading some stories," Luke explains as he looks up at me.

Once again, I'm entranced by his gaze. When I met him this morning, I forced myself to ignore it. After all, I needed to get out the door and to work with as little fuss as possible. Getting stuck in the morning rush would have ruined my whole day.

But now that I've got the time, I can truly appreciate Luke's beauty. What's more is that he looks truly at home as he sits beside Adrien. Like he belongs there.

In a lot of ways, he seems more like Adrien's dad than I do. I can't even get the kid to talk to me.

"Do you have to go now?" Adrien asks, looking up at Luke with a broken expression. Apparently, staying with me is absolutely the worst thing ever.

"Soon." Luke gives Adrien a little squeeze.

"Don't worry, he'll be back tomorrow. Won't you?" I shoot Luke a pleading look. Even from here I can see how much Adrien has changed since I left this morning. He still won't look at me, but his expression brightens when he looks up at Luke.

"Will you really?" Adrien asks. "Promise?"

Luke looks from me to Adrien and nods slowly. I think I catch a glimpse of relief in his eyes. "If you want me to come back, then I will."

"I do," Adrien says with a soft sigh. "I had a good day."

"I did too." Luke scoots toward the edge of the bed.

"And you'll read me this story tomorrow?"

"I will." His grin is completely natural as he looks from Adrien to me. "Or, Soren could read it to you now, if you want."

My heart freezes at his words. I don't think I'm ready for this. I've never actually read to a kid before. Is there anything special I need to do?

"I'll wait." Adrien closes the book and crawls under his covers.

I should have known there was nothing to worry about. It would've been more of a surprise if he actually said yes.

Luke gives me an apologetic smile and puts the book on Adrien's nightstand.

"I'll be here bright and early tomorrow morning," Luke says as he steps back from the bed.

"Will you leave the light on again?" Adrien asks.

"Yup." Luke walks toward me. "I'll do that right now."

"You'll make sure it stays on?" Adrien still doesn't look at me, but I can tell he's concerned that I'll do something wrong.

"Absolutely." Luke nods in reassurance. "I'll show Soren our trick so he knows."

Adrien doesn't look confident in my ability to comprehend whatever trick Luke is talking about, but he finally sinks down against his pillows. "Okay."

Luke turns off the room light and I back out into the hallway, feeling more like a third wheel than anything else. "Get some sleep and we'll go to the playground after breakfast, okay?"

"Good night, Luke," Adrien calls out as Luke steps away from the doorway.

"Good night, Adrien. Sleep tight." Luke leaves the bedroom door ajar slightly so the light from the hallway spills into the room. Is that what he meant by leaving the light on?

Luke nods toward the living room, and I follow him without question.

"Wow, I'm honestly impressed," I admit once we're in the kitchen. "He's like a completely different kid."

"I didn't really do much." Luke crosses his arms over his chest and frowns. "In fact, he hasn't really changed at all. He's just...coping a little better, I think."

"Coping?"

Luke narrows his eyes as if he can't believe what he's hearing. "How would you take it if the only family you've ever known dropped you off with a complete stranger and didn't even bother to pack your toothbrush?"

"Well...I mean, I know he's having a tough time. I just..." I quickly look for ways to salvage the conversation, but nothing feels right. "I just don't know what to do for him. I don't even know how to talk to him."

"You talk to him like a person." Luke relaxes his arms and smiles, seeming to lose some of his frustration. "He's five, not two. He can understand and communicate almost as well as you and me."

"I guess I just don't know how to act around kids. It's been a while since I've been around anyone that age." I look away, embarrassed by my own shortcomings.

"Actually, there's something else I wanted to talk to you about," Luke says, slipping further into the kitchen and glancing toward the hallway. His voice drops into something just above a whisper. "I'm concerned about what Adrien's life was like when he was living with your ex."

"What do you mean?" I move in close enough to hear properly, and to smell his enticing scent. Although the scent part is a bonus and the hearing part is just an excuse.

"Some things he said raised a few red flags for me..." Luke is picking his words carefully, and he keeps looking toward the hallway. "I'm not calling it straight-out abuse...at least, not physical. Emotional maybe...but I'm not an expert on this sort of thing. And really, I'm not trained to help a kid overcome the kind of trauma that abandonment creates. Let alone dealing with all the other crap I've started picking up on."

"You told him you're coming back..."

"And I intend to," Luke says hastily. "I'm just saying that it might be a good idea to look into finding a therapist who specializes in early childhood emotional trauma. Someone who can help him, and us, better deal with everything."

Fuck, I didn't realize it was that bad. In the other room, my son is sleeping. A week ago, I never would've even dreamed this scenario was possible. Now, my annoyance at my ex is quickly morphing into a cold rage.

"I'll see what I can do." I nod and lean against the kitchen counter. "I know a few people in that field. I'll see if they know of anyone who can help."

Luke seems satisfied with that response, and a broad smile touches his lips. "Good. I was worried you might be one of those alphas who doesn't believe in therapy or something."

"I'll be the first person to admit I don't know anything about emotional trauma or processing difficult things." I shake my head and stare at the floor. "If I'm being perfectly honest, I've lived a pretty charmed life. I mean, I've worked hard to get where I am, and it definitely hasn't been easy, but I don't have a troubled past to relate to. Things have always, more or less, worked out the way I planned. I'm almost exactly where I thought I would be at this point in my life."

Luke breathes out a surprised laugh. "Good to know that life works out for some people."

"My point is that I'm fully aware that my situation is the exception rather than the rule." I fold my arms, feeling oddly defensive. "I'm willing to do everything

I can to make sure Adrien has the same advantages I did."

Luke is silent for a moment before replying. "I think all Adrien wants right now is a dad who sticks around."

7

———

LUKE

"You don't have to eat so fast."

Adrien practically inhales the waffles I just finished cutting up for him.

I've officially made it through a full week of employment. It's not my longest stint ever, but it's definitely getting close. With each passing day, I get a little more hopeful. Maybe this time, I won't have to say goodbye to a kid who's already worming his way into my heart.

Speaking of which, Adrien's put on a little weight. He was definitely too skinny before so the changes are a relief, and his complexion is a lot better now too. It's amazing what a few days of sunshine and good food will do for a kid. Not only that, but he seems to be coming out of his shell a bit more.

Yesterday was his first appointment with a counselor. According to Soren, it went pretty well, but I get the feeling he was upset by some of the stuff the session revealed. I'm guessing Adrien's other dad was an even worse parent than I initially imagined. It's amazing that Adrien is as calm and well behaved as he is, considering who raised him.

Today is Soren's day off which was supposed to be my day off too, but if I'm being perfectly honest, there's nowhere else I'd rather be. I don't have much waiting for me at home, and I want to earn as much goodwill as I can with Soren. We're already a good way into the month, and I'm due to need an emergency day off any time now.

"Something smells good," Soren announces as he sleepily enters the kitchen.

I've never seen him this casual before, and I like it. In comfy mismatched PJs, his hair askew, and bleary-eyed, he's just as attractive as when he's all made up with his pressed suits and carefully styled hair. It feels more genuine. Like I'm getting to see the real Soren.

And I like what I see.

"There's a plate for you, if you want it." I offer him a smile and nod toward the counter where I left a stack of waffles.

Soren grins at me. "I didn't realize I was getting a home chef when I hired you."

"I don't do this for everyone." I glance back at Adrien who is fully engrossed with his breakfast at the dining table. "Just the people I like."

Soren grabs his plate but remains in the kitchen, leaning against the counter. He's still trying to figure out how to act around Adrien. I've seen the desire there. He clearly wants to make some sort of connection with his son, but he doesn't know where to start. And with everything that Adrien's been through, I think he's worried about somehow making things worse.

"What are your plans for the day?" Soren asks after a few moments of silence. When he looks at me, a chill runs down my spine. I'm probably reading too much into it, but for a second, I could almost feel him undressing me with his eyes.

"We were going to the park, but the forecast says it's supposed to rain." I frown as I pull out my phone and open up the weather app. "Looks like we're expecting some sort of cold snap too."

"It's a little late in the year for that." Soren's gaze drifts over to Adrien. "But if you guys can't go to the park, then I guess we'll have to do something inside."

Adrien doesn't look up at him, still focused on polishing off the last few pieces of waffle from his plate.

"What would you like to do, Adrien?" I ask, gently encouraging him to weigh in on our plans for the day. It seems like he's used to just being dragged around everywhere and never being able to choose anything for himself. When left to his own devices, he usually chooses to play his video game or watch cartoons.

Adrien slowly looks up from his plate and casts a wary glance at Soren. When he turns back to me, there's a tentative look in his eye. "Can we use the paints?" Adrien's voice is barely audible as he speaks.

"That sounds fun," I agree enthusiastically. "Put your dirty plate by the sink and go get them, okay?"

Adrien's expression brightens as he slides off his chair and picks up the empty plate. He trots happily to the kitchen, steps up onto the stool by the sink, and puts his plate with the rest of the dishes waiting to be washed. Without a second's hesitation, he darts off to find the paint set we bought the other day.

"That's the most animated I've seen him get about anything." Soren sounds impressed.

"He's been opening up little by little." I rise from my chair and carry my plate to the sink. Flipping on the water, I reach for the sponge, but Soren grabs it first.

"Let me." His warm breath bounces off my neck as he hovers behind me. He's not actually touching me, but he's close enough that I can almost feel him. Heat radiates off his skin and that deep, sexy voice of his sends shivers down my spine.

"I was just going to put them in the dishwasher." I inhale as slowly as possible, trying to retain control of myself. "It'll only take a few minutes."

"You're not our maid." Soren's voice is playful but still so close I can barely stand it. "You're here to look after Adrien."

"I...I'm..." Words fail me as I fight to keep my eyes focused on the dirty dishes in front me. My cock is stirring from Soren's presence alone, and my cheeks are starting to flush.

"I've got the paints," Adrien announces from the direction of the living room. He rarely raises his voice for anything, let alone to assert himself.

I eagerly break away from Soren's overwhelming presence and regain my self-control. I can't let myself get carried away. Especially not with my condition. "Perfect!" I turn to look toward the living room where Adrien has already set out his paint set and the special book of watercolor coloring pages we bought. "I'll get a cup of water, and we can get started."

Before I can react, Soren's already handing me a glass of water and turning back to the kitchen sink. He quietly begins scrubbing the dishes as if nothing has happened.

And maybe nothing has.

Maybe I'm just reading too much into these brief moments. Maybe my racing pulse and flushed skin are just consequences of how long it's been since I've had an intimate relationship.

But, even as I join Adrien at the coffee table in the living room, I'm fully aware of Soren's every movement in the kitchen. My mind won't stop conjuring crazy scenarios in which Soren feels the same intensity in the air between us as I do.

8

SOREN

IT'S JUST ME, I'm sure of it.

I was sending some pretty clear signals just now, and I got zero response back from Luke. Which is probably for the best. Given my track record with men, anything more than a friendship is bound to end in broken hearts.

And now more than ever, I can't risk that.

Glancing into the living room, I see Luke and Adrien painting and chatting about something they watched on TV. Without Luke, I'm sure Adrien wouldn't be adjusting as well as he is.

I take my time rinsing the dishes and loading the dishwasher. This is the first time in my life that I've had to put someone else first. My decisions don't just affect me anymore. Now, I've got to think about Adrien and what's best for him. He's had so much instability and neglect in his life.

I need to make up for all the time I wasn't there to protect him.

The appointment with the counselor, or therapist or whatever they're called, didn't reveal much. They told me it would take time for Adrien to get comfortable with me and that there might be things we'd never get the full scope of. One thing that came out rather easily was that he doesn't think of me as his dad and clearly resents having to live with me.

Obviously, I already know that.

But I'm hopeful that with patience, stability, and love, he'll start to adjust to this new situation. It's going to take time, but I'm willing to wait for him to come around.

Once I finish loading the dishwasher, I hover awkwardly in the kitchen for another moment. As much as I'd like to join them, Adrien always clams up when I'm around. Right now, he seems perfectly happy to be educating Luke on how to properly color trees.

But I can't avoid him forever.

Taking a deep breath, I step boldly into the living room and head toward the sofa. Adrien looks up at me as I approach, but he doesn't stop talking to Luke.

"I like green trees but sometimes they're red or brown." Adrien returns his gaze to the page where he's been carefully applying the watercolors.

I'm actually impressed with the effort he's putting into his artwork. It never occurred to me that kids his age could do anything other than finger paint.

"I've seen pink trees before," Luke says, adding to the conversation. "They're really pretty."

"One time, I saw a purple tree." Adrien is very excited as he talks. He launches into vivid descriptions of different types of trees and their colors. Well, as vivid as possible for someone who's still developing their vocabulary.

Awkwardly, I take a seat on the sofa a few feet away from where Adrien and Luke are painting. I don't want to intrude on their fun, and I'm not really sure I'd be much use anyway. I can't remember the last time I did anything that could be considered "creative."

Luke's eyes are on me as I pull out my phone and start to check my email. He probably wants me to join them on the floor, but I don't think that's a good idea yet.

For now, I think it's enough that we're all in the same room together, and Adrien is actually opening up and engaging in something he enjoys. To the outside observer, the three of us probably look like a little happy family.

That thought makes my heart thrum as I turn back to Luke.

He hastily looks away and focuses on the half-painted page in front of him.

Family isn't something I've thought about in a really long time. On the rare occasion that I actually have a boyfriend, my thoughts are never on the long-term. Maybe that's why those relationships always fizzle out the moment the sex gets boring or things get a little too intense.

Maybe if I go into a relationship looking for a mate, things could be different?

As if reading my thoughts, Luke meets my gaze. He might not have responded strongly when we were in the kitchen, but I'm starting to think that might have just been a front for Adrien's benefit. Because right now, the look he's giving me makes me want to take him straight to the bedroom.

I clear my throat and force myself to look back down at my email inbox.

"What's your favorite color?" Luke asks as Adrien's long explanation about trees slowly dies out. His question is just the thing to keep Adrien engaged, and the two of them continue their conversation.

Meanwhile, I sort through the endless messages piling up in my inbox. Even when I'm out of the office, work never really stops. It's just part of the job when you're at my level. There's always more that needs to be done, and there just aren't enough hours in the week.

Makes me wonder why I even want a promotion and all the extra work that will come with it.

For the most part, I can respond to most of my messages without having to look anything up. There are a few that can wait until I'm back in the office tomorrow. One, however, catches my eye immediately.

It's from my boss, Robert. The subject line reads "Promotion?"

Heart pounding, I open up the email.

Looking forward to hearing your decision soon. I'm sure you've already shopped around a bit. You're not going to get an offer like this anywhere else.

It's a not so subtle hint that the timer on the offer is running out. I've only got a few more days to give him my answer, and I'm no closer to a decision than I was when he first told me. In fact, I'm even more unsure now than I was.

"What are you frowning about?" Luke asks, interrupting my thoughts.

I look up to find both him and Adrien staring at me. "Oh, just an email from my boss. Nothing to worry about." I force a smile and put my phone away.

"Are you getting fired?" Adrien asks abruptly.

I blink in surprise. I'm pretty sure this is the first time he's addressed me directly. "Um...no, I'm not. My boss wants to give me a better job, actually."

"My dad looked like that whenever he got fired." Adrien looks back to his painting. "He wasn't ever happy."

"I'm happy." I smile to emphasize my point. "It's just not an easy decision. If I take this new job, then I'll have to be at work more often."

Luke is watching us quietly but seems to be intentionally staying out of our exchange.

"You're at work all the time anyway." Adrien picks up his paintbrush and continues his work. He doesn't seem to be aware of just how deeply his comment hits me.

Luke purses his lips and shrugs. Clearly, they both agree that I'm gone more often than I should be.

"Would it be better if I was home more?" I ask, slowly looking back at Adrien.

No response.

Seems he's shutting me out again. I'm simultaneously encouraged and disheartened. He opens up just long enough to tell me I'm never around and then goes silent again.

My gaze drops back down to my phone. It's not something that needs my attention right this second. I've still got time to figure things out. What's important right now is making an effort to let Adrien know I'm going to be here for him when it counts.

Swallowing my anxiousness, I slowly slide off the sofa and take up a position alongside one edge of the coffee table.

"So, which one of you wants to show me how this works?" I look directly at Adrien, hoping he takes the bait. "I don't know the first thing about painting."

Adrien studies me for a moment, and I'm almost certain he's going to get up and walk away, but he surprises me by ripping a page out of the coloring book and sliding it toward me.

My heart leaps in victory. It's not much, but it's enough for now.

9

———

LUKE

By mid-morning, it's pouring down rain outside, and I'm dreading the trip home. There's nothing worse than sitting on the bench in the rain and then riding the bus home soaked to the bone.

Especially when the apartment is nice and cozy, and the smell of hot cocoa is wafting through the air. I decided to go old school and make it from scratch the way my grandma used to when I was a kid. The instant powder stuff just isn't the same, not that Soren would even keep that junk in his cupboards.

Every now and then, there's a murmur from the living room as either Soren or Adrien tries to start a conversation. Neither of them are very good at small talk, but they're making progress at least. All it took was a bit of watercolor and a couple of puzzles.

They're currently putting together a big 100-piece puzzle featuring one of Adrien's favorite cartoons. I'm pretty sure Adrien's never put a puzzle together before, and Soren was quite happy to be able to teach him how it's done.

Once he got the hang of it, Adrien took to it like a champ.

I ladle out the cocoa into some oversized coffee mugs and delicately carry them into the living room. I've already tested it to make sure it's not too hot, and it's the perfect level of sweetness. I can't wait to see what Adrien thinks of it.

"Is that coffee?" Adrien wrinkles his nose as I set the mugs down on the table. "It doesn't smell like coffee."

"It's hot chocolate." Soren gleefully takes the mug I offer him. "It's the perfect way to warm up on a day like today."

"Cuz I don't like coffee." Adrien is still skeptical as he gingerly lifts the mug. "My dad loves coffee."

"Well, this isn't coffee, so I think you'll like it." I wink, encouraging him to give it a try.

Soren is already sipping his drink, but I can tell by his expression that he's stewing again. Every time Adrien mentions his dad, Soren flinches slightly. It definitely bothers him that Adrien still has such a strong attachment to a man who didn't care for him properly.

Thankfully, he does a good job at masking his disappointment. If I wasn't constantly ogling that chiseled jaw and strong brow of his, I probably wouldn't pick up on it so often.

Adrien mimics Soren's actions, sipping at the edge of the mug to get a little taste of the chocolatey goodness inside.

"Mmmm, this is really good!" Adrien's face lights up, and he looks at me with wide-eyed wonder.

"I made it just the way my grandma used to." I breathe in the familiar scent and smile. "She used to make it for me all the time when I was your age."

Adrien takes a deep drink this time. "It's nice and warm too." He's grinning from ear to ear and my heart melts a bit at the sight. "We don't have this at my house."

Soren takes a big drink from his mug, probably to keep from saying something he shouldn't.

"I'm glad you like it." I lean back and look at the puzzle that's spread across the table. "You guys got a lot done while I was in the kitchen."

"You were hogging all the straight pieces," Adrien says simply.

"He's right." Soren looks at me and nods. "When you got up, we realized all the pieces we needed for the border were in your pile there."

I open my mouth to protest and see them both staring at me. "Really? All of them?"

"Most of them." Adrien points to a huge section of the puzzle. "But we got it figured out." He puts his half-empty mug down on the table and snaps another piece into place. "You just gotta not do that next time."

Properly scolded, I agree to do better. "Right, I'll try harder next time."

Adrien stifles a yawn before picking up his cocoa mug again. "I'm not tired."

"It's okay if you are," Soren says, yawning widely. "A nap sounds pretty good right now."

"I don't want to nap, though." Adrien hurriedly picks up a few more puzzle pieces and puts them together. "I don't want to."

"Why don't we finish our cocoa and this puzzle first?" I pick up a piece and try in an open gap, but it doesn't fit. "Maybe when we're done, we can all take a little nap?"

Adrien cocks his head and frowns. "You guys are gonna nap too?"

"I am, that's for sure." Soren stretches and lets out another exaggerated yawn.

"Luke?" Adrien looks at me.

"I am pretty tired, I guess." I've taken a few power naps on the sofa over the past week but never while Soren's been home. I don't know why, but I'm actually excited by the idea of sleeping while he's so close.

Satisfied with our answers, Adrien returns to his careful examination of the puzzle pieces on the table that still need to be placed. He grabs a few more pieces and tries to find the spots where they belong.

Every now and then, Soren or I will add in a piece to keep things moving.

Technically, we could have finished it a while ago, but we seem to have reached an unspoken agreement to let Adrien lead the charge. Every time he finds a successful match, he beams with pride, and his smile makes my heart swell.

When the last piece is in place, Adrien looks at us in triumph. "We did it!" He holds up the puzzle box and shows us the picture. "It matches perfect."

"High-fives for everyone." I hold up one hand toward Adrien and the other toward Soren. I get my high-fives and then, to my complete surprise, Adrien turns to Soren and high-fives him too.

"Good job, everyone," Soren says, clearly trying not to make a big deal out of the gesture. "That was a tough one."

"It was really hard," Adrien agrees. "But I liked it a lot."

"Maybe we'll get some more puzzles soon then," Soren says.

Adrien looks up at him in surprise and smiles.

As much as I don't want to butt into their moment, this is the perfect teachable moment for Soren about how to negotiate with his son. "Maybe that can be your reward if you start brushing your teeth every morning." It's been a struggle to get Adrien to keep up with that habit.

Adrien wrinkles his nose at that suggestion.

"That's a really good idea." Soren nods and clasps his hands together. "If you brush your teeth every morning for seven days, we'll get another puzzle. How does that sound?"

Adrien purses his lips thoughtfully, clearly not thrilled with the idea, but he relents without putting up much of a fight. "Okay, deal."

"Now, it's nap time," I remind him as I collect the empty mugs from the table.

"Just a short nap." Adrien stands up and tries to hide a yawn. "Not a long one."

"I'll take those." Soren reaches for the mugs as I start to carry them to the kitchen.

"It's fine. I'll just put them in the dishwasher. Why don't you get Adrien tucked in?" I shoot him a little smile of reassurance.

Adrien looks at Soren but doesn't say anything.

"I...I can do that." Soren clears his throat, obviously not very confident but willing to give it a try. "You'll have to tell me what to do, though, Adrien."

"It's not that hard." Adrien rolls his eyes. "Come on."

"I can't tell," Soren whispers close to me once Adrien is down the hall. "Is he okay with this? He doesn't seem thrilled."

"Yes, this is good." I chuckle and nod toward Adrien's room. "Go on now."

Soren pulls back his shoulders and heads off to tuck his son in for the first time. The nervous excitement on his face is almost contagious. Finally, after all this time, he gets to do something that normal dads get to do every day.

We're not there yet, but there's a faint light forming at the end of this tunnel.

10

SOREN

"Does he always want you to read that many stories?" I ask Luke as we slip out of Adrien's room and into the hallway. "I didn't think he'd ever fall asleep."

"I usually cut him off after two or three." Luke grins at the fact that I was suckered into six whole books. "After a certain point, he's fighting to stay awake just to get more stories."

I adjust the door so the hallway light provides some light into his room. There's a nightlight next to Adrien's bed now, but we still leave the light on so he can see if he needs to get up.

We head into the living room where the puzzle is still laid out on the table and the watercolor pages are on the floor, drying in a spot that's out of the way. It's still hard to believe I just spent the whole morning actually connecting with my kid. To be perfectly honest, I was kinda dreading my first day off.

Now, I'm starting to resent that I'll have to go back to work tomorrow.

"Thank you for this." I gesture to the completed puzzle. "I was completely lost before you came into our lives. I probably would've made things worse if it weren't for your help."

"Give yourself a little credit." He blushes and shakes his head. "You're better at the dad thing than you think."

It means a lot to hear him say that. I don't exactly have an abundance of confidence in that area.

"Geez, the rain just won't stop." Luke shifts the topic of conversation, crossing to the window on the far side of the room. "It's ridiculous."

Dropping heavily onto the sofa, I realize how tired I actually feel. I wasn't just joking when I told Adrien I wanted to take a nap too.

"What do you usually do when he's sleeping?" I ask, fighting the urge to yawn.

"Sleep." Luke laughs and takes a spot on the other end of the sofa.

I'm painfully aware of the emptiness between us right now. All morning long, I've had to fight my urge to close the distance. Now that Adrien's asleep in the other room, it's even harder to hold back.

"I'm not really a morning person," Luke admits. "These early mornings have been a killer."

"I'm not exactly a fan of them either." I turn slightly to face him. "But those early-morning staff meetings aren't something I can afford to miss."

"Are you going to take that promotion?" Luke asks with an unreadable look in his eyes.

"I don't know..." I shake my head, frustrated by the timing of everything. "It's a massive pay increase and a huge step up for my career. Two weeks ago, I wouldn't have hesitated...but now..." I glance toward the hallway.

He doesn't let me off the hook. "Now?"

"Now, I'm starting to question everything." I take a deep breath before locking eyes with Luke. "What Adrien said about me never being home is true. It wasn't a problem when it was just me, but now I've got to think about him too. He's never going to think of me as his dad if I'm never home."

"You're right." Luke is a straight shooter, for sure. He doesn't even pretend like taking the promotion is a good idea.

I lapse into silence. There's no easy answer here. No matter how I twist it in my head, I can't make the promotion work. Not without sacrificing my home-life entirely. That's something I just can't afford to do anymore.

"Do you have a decision?" Luke asks as if reading my thoughts.

"For starters, I'm going to turn down the promotion." I sit up straighter and try to order my thoughts. "I'm still figuring things out after that."

"Well, I'll be here for as long as you need me." Luke smiles and my mind goes blank.

"I'll always need you." The words just fell from my lips without any approval from my brain. Luke's eyes grow wide, and I immediately panic. "I mean, we. We'll always need you. Adrien and me. Like I said, we wouldn't have gotten this far without you."

"It's only been a week." Luke waves away the compliment, trying to play it off with a light laugh. "I'm sure any good babysitter would've been able to do the same."

I'm silent for a long moment as I watch him fidgeting beneath my gaze. He's picking at his fingernails, and the way his hair falls across his forehead and into his eyes makes me want to reach out and brush it back for him. And then I'd cup his face in my hands and gently press my lips to his...

My cheeks grow hot as my thoughts begin to wander into the gutter. Didn't I just resolve not to go down this path? I can't start something with Luke. At the very least, I can't rush into something with him.

"I think you're selling yourself short." I finally shift my gaze away from him and look out the window.

"Arlo watched Adrien a few times before you came, and he didn't make much headway. Adrien trusts you, and so do I."

Luke's head snaps up in surprise. "I...I'm glad." His throat flexes, and his voice is thick with emotion. "It means a lot to hear you say that."

Before I can reply, I'm overcome by a yawn. "Excuse me, sorry," I mumble as I try to contain a second yawn. "I guess that whole nap idea kinda got me thinking about sleep."

"That makes two of us." Luke curls his legs up under himself before yawning.

"You can use my bed if you'd like," I offer without hesitation. "I'll use the sofa. I doubt I'll sleep long."

"Oh, no thanks." Luke shakes his head in protest. "I'm used to napping out here."

I quickly rack my brain for something to say, but my head is a foggy mess of naughty scenes that definitely wouldn't be appropriate to share.

"If you stick around too long, I'll end up using you as a pillow." Luke opens his eyes enough to wink playfully. He scoots a bit closer to me to lend weight to his threat.

"I'm not sure I'd make the best pillow." Despite my warning, I don't move an inch. "You'd probably be more comfortable in the other room."

"Nah, I think this will work just fine." Luke is suddenly at my side and resting his head on my shoulder. "You're a better pillow than you might think."

"I'm not sure how much sleep you're going to get like that." My heart is pounding against my rib cage, and my cock is begging me to do something, anything to relieve it from my pants. The best I can do is shift my position and cross my legs.

I refuse to let my dick do the talking right now.

"Want me to go get you a real pillow?" I'm more comfortable than I can ever remember being but I can't imagine Luke likes my hard shoulder under his cheek. "If you're determined to sleep out here, that's the least I can do."

There's no answer from Luke.

I crane my head slightly to get a look at his face. His eyes are closed, and his face is completely relaxed. His breathing is slow and steady. I think he really is asleep already.

It takes all my willpower not to gently stroke his cheek as he sleeps. He looks so perfect, so peaceful.

Sinking back against the couch cushions, I hesitantly rest my head against his. This wasn't exactly what I expected when I mentioned taking a nap, but I'm definitely not complaining.

I WAKE up with a start as the TV flickers to life. It takes me a minute to process my surroundings.

I'm still in the living room at Soren's apartment, and Adrien is sitting on the floor by the coffee table, with his video game controller in hand.

He looks back when he hears me stir and smiles. "Did you have a good nap?"

"I think so." I stifle a yawn and slowly sit up. My body is sore from the weird angle I was sleeping at.

My heart dives to my toes as I suddenly remember the last few minutes before falling asleep. I hadn't meant to actually fall asleep on Soren. I was just joking around with him, but by the time the joke should have ended, I must have already passed out.

Soren is slowly waking up beside me, and his beautiful lashes flutter as he rubs his eyes. "Well, hello, sleepyhead."

His dreamy smile makes my cock stir. My cheeks grow hot as I try to figure out what to say.

"Why are you so red?" Adrien asks, turning around to face us. "Are you sick?"

"N-no," I stammer. "I just..."

Before I can say anything else, Soren's hand presses against my forehead. His skin is cool against my flushed face, and it soothes me instantly. I almost shiver beneath his touch and silently wish I could stay like this forever

"No fever." Soren winks and offers a playful grin then withdraws his hand and bounces off the sofa with the energy of a child. "Just the sign of a restful nap."

I mask my disappointment at his departure with a fake pout. "I said I wasn't sick."

"Just wanted to make sure." Soren waggles his eyebrows at me before trotting toward the kitchen. "I think we all overslept a bit." He begins digging through the cupboards. "I'm starved."

My gaze snaps toward the window and I suddenly realize it's already dark outside. The clock on the wall shows it's well after seven PM.

"Wow, it's late." I rise from the sofa and stretch my aching muscles. "I should get going."

"I think you've already missed your bus." Soren starts to pile things on the counter as he prepares to make dinner. "Why don't you stay for dinner, and I'll drive you home after."

"I can get a rideshare." Despite wanting to take him up on his offer, I hate to drag him and Adrien out this late. "It's no trouble."

"If you'd rather not taste my cooking, all you have to do is say so." Soren's tone is teasing, and my body responds to this fun side of his. I haven't really experienced him like this, and I like it. "You don't have to make excuses."

To be perfectly honest, I have wanted to try out Soren's cooking for a while now. His assortment of ingredients is pretty high end, not to mention the quality cookware his kitchen is stocked with. I've been wondering if he's actually good in the kitchen or just likes to keep stuff around as decoration. "I'm not trying to avoid your cooking."

"Then stay." His eyes pierce me, and I can feel the command in those few letters.

"Please!" Adrien chimes in. "You can sit next to me."

"See?" Soren grins and nods toward his partner in crime. "You're outnumbered."

"Okay, okay." I hold up my hands in defeat. "You guys win. I'll stay for dinner."

"Yay!" Adrien cheers and turns back to his video game.

Soren, on the other hand, continues to hold me in place with his intense gaze for a few more seconds.

I can't look away from him, even if I wanted to...which I don't.

My breath is short, and my heart is thrumming in my chest. I want to get closer to him, but I resist. I've already overstepped my boundaries with the whole nap thing. My hormones are running wild in my veins right now, and I know what that means. It looks like I have no choice but to cash in those vacation days I add to every contract.

And all because I was being silly and let a dumb joke go too far.

Taking stock of how I feel, I'm confident I've got a few more hours before my body gets too out of hand. I'll apologize to Soren and explain everything to him when he takes me home.

Earlier, he said he trusts me. Hopefully, that will earn me a bit of leniency with this awkward and embarrassing situation.

For now, I just need to keep my shit together through dinner and avoid making any more mistakes.

As if reading my desperation for a distraction, Adrien shoves a video game controller into my hand and asks me to help him get through the level he's stuck on. Having something to focus on is exactly what I need to help me stay calm through the uncomfortable conversation that's waiting for me after dinner.

It's not long before an amazing aroma begins wafting out of the kitchen. Soren's cooking up a storm in there, and it's making my mouth water. Grandma always said to find myself an alpha who can cook.

What am I doing?

I forcibly clear my throat and refocus on the video game. I don't have an alpha. I have an employer who just happens to be a highly attractive alpha...who can cook. But he's not *my* alpha. I can't let myself think like that. That kind of thinking will get me into trouble and may even cost me my job.

Adrien is grinning from ear to ear as he tells me all about a hidden room he found in the game. I'm not the only one who will suffer if I lose this job. Adrien's had enough turmoil in his life, and he doesn't need to lose another person he's grown to trust.

By the time Soren calls us for dinner, I'm starting to regret sticking around. I've gotten very used to my body's signals, and I'm pretty sure that in less than two hours, I'll be morphing away from being a mild-mannered and perfectly polite omega, to a sex-crazed maniac with a scent that puts other omegas to shame.

If I don't get out of here before then…

No, I will not think about that.

Instead, I help Adrien set the table and wash his hands for dinner.

"Well? What do you think?" Soren waves his hands at the meal laid out before us.

"Looks like something out of a restaurant." I nod in appreciation as I sit down.

"It looks icky," Adrien says with a frown.

"I made yours special." Soren points at Adrien's plate. "There are no mushrooms on it. Just stuff that you like. It's all stuff you've eaten before, I promise."

"Are you sure?" Adrien climbs into his chair and pokes at his food.

"Use a fork, Adrien," I softly remind him of his manners. We've been working on them at every opportunity.

"Yes, I'm sure," Soren says to his son, taking his seat with a flourish. "You'll like it."

Adrien hesitantly picks up a fork and tests a bite. His face lights up, and a moment later, he's eagerly digging in.

"There we go." Soren smiles happily as he looks across the table at me. "Please, enjoy."

Soren actually does know how to cook, and he's pretty good at it too. The food is better than I expected. Maybe sticking around was worth the risk.

Glancing around the table, we actually look like a family right now. That thought fills my stomach with butterflies. A little family of three.

I didn't realize how badly I wanted something like that until right now. But this is just a daydream. A fantasy. After dinner, I'll go home to my little apartment, I'll go to sleep in the bed I share with no one, and I'll wake up and eat breakfast alone. As usual.

The ache in my chest is almost unbearable. This is just a job. This isn't some fantasyland where I get to play house and pretend I'm something I'm not. Adrien needs me to be there for him as a reliable babysitter. Pursuing my own silly ideas would be selfish. I can't do that to him.

No matter how much it hurts.

"It's pretty late," Soren says as we finish up dinner. "We should probably get going."

"Why don't we have a sleepover?" Adrien asks abruptly. "Then Luke doesn't have to go."

Alarms go off in my head, and I search my mind for a viable excuse.

Before I get a chance to speak, Soren jumps in. "It's up to Luke." His eyes lock with mine and there's a glint of excitement in them. "I'm sure we can give you a proper place to sleep if you do decide to stay the night."

"I...I really wish I could," I stammer to get the words out. "But...I need to get home."

"Aww..." Adrien pouts a little.

"Another time maybe." I force a smile and push back from the table. "Tonight isn't good for me."

"But why?" Adrien's brow furrows. "You guys were sleeping on the sofa. You like each other. So you should stay with us."

I blush deeply and look down into my lap. I don't have a good answer to give him, and I'm already torn between the two options. Everything in me wants to say yes, but I can't risk it.

"Adrien, why don't you go and get your coat and your shoes on?" Soren suggests. "Luke will come back tomorrow, but tonight, we're gonna take him home. Okay?"

I open my mouth to protest, but the words die on my lips.

"Fine." Adrien reluctantly slides from his chair and shuffles down the hallway to his room.

"I wish you hadn't said that..." I say as I look back at Soren.

"What? It's true, isn't it?" Soren frowns.

"I...um, well, I'm going to need to take one of those absences in my contract." I take a deep breath and look him in the eyes. "I know it's not great timing, and I really wish I didn't have to, but..."

"You're serious, aren't you?" Soren slowly rises from his chair and circles around the table toward me. "Is it because of earlier? Did I do something to make you uncomfortable? I never meant to."

I turn to face him and anguish fills my chest as I try to keep myself under control. The hormones flooding my body are bringing everything to the surface and time is not on my side. "It's not that at all." I shake my head emphatically. "I just...I have a medical condition. It's hard to explain."

"So, you really are sick?" Concern floods his features as he once again presses his hand to my forehead.

"No, not like that..." I glance toward the hallway and prepare for the inevitable. There's still no sign of Luke, so this is my chance. God knows I don't want to explain this in front of him.

Soren lowers his hand and kneels beside my chair. "What is it then? I told you how much we need you. Please help me understand what's going on."

From the look on his face it's clear that Soren still thinks I'm using this as an excuse to get away from him.

"I...I have a condition." I speak slowly, choosing my words carefully. "It makes it so that suppressants don't work on me."

"Suppressants?" Soren cocks his head, trying to figure out what the hell I'm talking about. "Wait...you mean? Suppressants? Those suppressants?" His eyes are wide with shock as the meaning sets in.

"Yes, those. So, for a few days out of every month, I can't be around anyone else. I've got to hole myself up at home and stay away from everyone." I bark out a rough laugh. "If I don't...well..."

"Right..." Soren rises to his feet and takes a few steps back. "And this is going to happen tomorrow?"

"Tonight, actually." I slide my chair farther back to put more distance between us. "That's why I wanted to leave earlier. I can feel it starting and I don't have much time to get out of here before things start to get...crazy. But I couldn't say no when Adrien asked me to stay." I close my eyes for a long moment and then look at him. "I'm sorry."

"Shit." Soren swears under his breath. "I wish you'd told me earlier. I wouldn't have pressured you into staying."

"I wanted to stay." I clear my throat and speak the words I shouldn't. "I still do. But..."

"Don't worry...we'll get you home." Soren reaches for his keys and slides them into his pocket. "You don't have to explain any more."

12

SOREN

Clouds of steam billow from my mouth as soon as I set foot outside. The air is bitterly cold, and it's still raining. An icy wind tears at my jacket as I shuffle forward, ushering Luke and Adrien out of the apartment.

The walkway to the parking lot is well lit, but we only go a few feet before I slip and nearly lose my balance. A sheet of ice has already formed across the pavement, and now that I'm looking for it, I can see it glistening in the lamplight.

"How is it this cold?" I mutter as I regain my footing. "Be careful. The ice is slippery."

I take one of Adrien's hands, and Luke takes the other. Together, the three of us carefully walk to the parking lot.

We're only halfway there when a sound like a gunshot rips through the air. A massive branch snaps free from one of the trees near the parking lot and crashes to the pavement just inches from several parked cars.

A few steps farther and that would have hit one or all of us.

I look back at Luke and Adrien. They're huddling behind me, fear in their eyes.

If branches that big are coming down, it's not safe out here, and it's certainly not safe on the roads. I'm not going to risk our lives.

"Back inside." I turn and guide them back down the path toward home.

"Soren..." Luke's voice is filled with fear.

"I know. Don't worry." I keep my eyes fixed on the path ahead. I have no idea how we're going to handle Luke's situation, but it's too dangerous to risk the road.

As soon as everyone is safely back inside, I pull up the weather report on my phone.

"I guess we should've checked this earlier." I shake my head, annoyed with myself for not being more vigilant. Normally, I'm at least aware of this kind of thing.

"What's it say?" Luke asks as he helps Adrien out of his coat.

"Freezing rain all night long. With a warning to watch out for icy roads and falling trees." I look up and realize that, despite his jacket, Adrien's soaked.

In fact, we all are.

"Can you help Adrien into the tub?" I kick off my soaking wet shoes and peel off my socks. "I'll lend you some dry clothes and swap out with you once I get changed."

Luke swallows hard and then nods. "Yeah, okay. Come on, Adrien. Let's get you warmed up."

"Does this mean we're having a sleepover?" Adrien asks with a newfound excitement toward sleeping.

Luke and I exchange a glance. The worry in his eyes is evident, but he doesn't let Adrien catch on. "Yeah, I guess it does. Come on. A warm bath will be perfect right now."

Adrien jumps up and down, more childlike than I've ever seen him. "Will you read me a story before bed? Can you sleep in my room? My bed's big enough!"

He pesters Luke with questions as they head to the bathroom.

Down the hall in my bedroom, I try to gather my thoughts as I change out of my wet clothes. The clock is ticking, and Luke will go into heat soon. Honestly, I don't know what to expect when that happens. I've never actually been around an omega in heat before.

At least, not one that wasn't also on suppressants.

I mean, I know what I learned in sex ed back in high school, but that was a filtered version of reality. Once an omega goes into heat, it can last several days. And the scent of an omega in heat will cause intense arousal in any sexually mature alpha who smells it. That's pretty much all I remember, but that's enough.

Because this apartment isn't big enough for me to avoid smelling Luke's scent...or for him to avoid me.

Fortunately, Adrien's still too young to even notice because that sense doesn't develop until after puberty. But not being able to properly explain what's happening might make the next few days even harder for us all.

Digging through my dresser, I find some pajamas that never fit me well, so they might fit Luke. I toss them onto the bed, then quickly change into something dry.

For now, the best I can do is lock Luke in my room. In the morning, we can try to get him home safely. No idea how that's going to work, but I have all night to figure it out.

Of course, there's another solution that we haven't considered yet. My mouth goes dry at the thought of potentially "helping" Luke with this unexpected problem.

But I can't suggest something like that. Luke made it clear that he wants to go home and lock himself away. There's no way I can just offer to knot him...can I?

No. No, I cannot.

Squaring my shoulders, I head to the bathroom where Luke is in the middle of washing Adrien's hair.

"I laid out some clothes for you. They're probably too big, but it's better than being soaked all night." I lean against the door frame and watch the two people who occupy one hundred percent of my focus.

"Thanks." Luke glances back at me and offers a small smile. "Do you want to get Adrien's PJs while I finish up here?"

"Get the dinosaur ones," Adrien says.

"Please." Luke uses his teaching voice to remind my son about his manners.

"Please," Adrien repeats, looking up at me with a smile.

"Right away." I jog to Adrien's room and dig through his dresser for the requested pajamas. By the time I get back, Luke has him wrapped in a big fluffy towel and is helping him dry his hair.

"I can get dressed by myself." Adrien holds on to his towel tightly as I pass the pajamas to Luke.

"Okay, you do that." Luke sets the clothes on the floor nearby and steps toward the doorway. "I'm gonna go get changed too."

"Then will you read to me?"

"Actually, I think Soren wants to read to you tonight." Luke's tone is back to soft and gentle.

"He read to me earlier."

"Why don't you get dressed, and then we'll talk about it, okay?" Even though Luke can handle the situation better thanI can, I intervene so he can excuse himself. "Luke needs to get out of those wet clothes."

"Okay..." Adrien sighs but doesn't put up too much of a fuss.

Luke follows me out into the hallway as Adrien gets changed.

"How are you doing?" I ask, keeping my voice low.

"I'm fine for now." I can hear the uncertainty in his voice as Luke keeps his eyes averted. "But that could change at any minute now."

I nod and keep several feet of space between us. "When the time comes, you can lock yourself in my bedroom. I'll tell Adrien you're not feeling well."

"That won't be far from the truth." Luke chokes out a laugh but I can hear how miserable he is. He shifts his gaze to meet mine. "I don't think you understand just how bad this is going to be. Suppressants don't work on me because of just how strong my scent is. Using a suppressant would just make it the same as a normal omega without them."

"What do you want me to do?" The words I want to say are on the tip of my tongue but I hold them back. If he wants to make the suggestion, that's his call. "You saw what it's like out there."

"I know, I know..." Luke shakes his head and wraps his arms around his torso. "I'm just trying to prepare you. Locking me in the bedroom might not be enough to contain the scent."

Adrien is humming in the bathroom as he gets his PJs on.

"We've got to take this one step at a time." I shrug and hope he feels comfortable enough to be honest about what he needs from me. Whatever that might be. "For now, just get changed. There's not much else we can do at the moment."

Luke nods and takes a deep breath. "Okay. I just...I'm sorry. I'm not trying to sound ungrateful. I know this isn't something you were expecting to deal with."

"You don't have to apologize." I smile and wave away his concerns. "You haven't done anything wrong. I'm serious."

He returns my smile but it's not sincere. Then he turns into the bedroom, locking the door behind him.

Adrien appears at my side with a book in hand. "I'm ready."

"Let's get your teeth brushed first." I nod back toward the bathroom.

Adrien hops up onto the step stool by the sink without protest.

I'm not sure how independent he is with his hygiene, but I've seen Luke help with these kind of things, so

I squeeze out a little toothpaste onto the bristles of his toothbrush and hand it to him.

"Do you love Luke?" Adrien asks as he looks at himself in the mirror.

"Luke's our friend." My heart skips a beat, and I force myself to laugh to cover up my embarrassment. "Do you know what love is?"

"It's when someone kisses you and sleeps in your bed with you." Adrien shrugs like that is the obvious answer. "My dad had lots of friends that he loved."

I have to bite my tongue to keep from saying something I shouldn't. "Well, love is more than just that. When you really love someone, they become part of your family forever."

Adrien looks down at his toothbrush. "So they never leave?"

I hesitate to answer because I can tell he's struggling to make sense of everything that's happened to him. "Sometimes, even when we love someone, we can't stay with them." I wish I knew how to properly help him, but all I can hope for is to not screw him up even more. "But even if we can't be with the people we love, it doesn't mean that we don't love them anymore."

"Oh..." Adrien looks up at me and studies my face carefully.

"Scoot over. I need to brush my teeth too." I grab my toothbrush and start applying the toothpaste. "You can tell me if I'm doing it wrong. Okay?"

Adrien grins at me. "Okay."

13
———

LUKE

SHIT!

The expletives racing through my head are loud and numerous.

I should've gotten out sooner. I shouldn't have stayed for dinner. Adrien would've been disappointed, but I could've apologized later. Now, I'm having a mini meltdown in Soren's bedroom as I strip out of my wet clothing.

But being in here is actually pushing me into my heat even faster. I can smell Soren on everything in this room. The pungent, musky, heady scent of an alpha.

It's driving me crazy and kicking my hormones into overdrive. Time isn't on our side.

With my wet clothes in a pile by the door, I stand beside Soren's bed and take in a deep breath. My skin prickles with goosebumps, making me shiver against the warm air of the apartment. Exposed like this, surrounded by his scent, I can't suppress the arousal that's beginning to course through me.

My cock is already hard as I shudder beside the bed.

The first whiff of my heat reaches my nose, and I know I'm done for. It's a good thing I locked the bedroom door when I came in here, because it'll only be a matter of minutes before Soren catches my scent.

Soren laid out clean clothes for me, so I reach for the shirt and pull it on. As the fabric touches my skin, I moan with desire. Soren's scent envelopes me as the oversized shirt settles across my thighs. It's long enough that it could almost be a night-gown on me, and I don't want to wear anything but this.

My aching cock brushes against the shirt, forming an obvious tent. In the full-length mirror hanging on the back of the bedroom door, I take a moment to see what I look like to Soren.

If he could see me right now, would he like the view?

The thought stirs in my brain and makes me twitch with desire. It's a struggle to keep my mind from running wild. Especially because I was already attracted to Soren before this whole thing started, and I'm pretty sure he's been flirting with me all day too.

Then why all this pretense? The horny, primal part of my brain wants me to give in to my desires. Why am I trying to hide myself away? It's just going to make us both miserable. And it's not like I can stay locked up in here for however long it takes for this to end.

That's not only unrealistic but I'll have to eat and use the bathroom at some point.

But...is he still going to like me when this is over? Will he still want me around? My relationship with Adrien is too important to risk the messiness of an intimate relationship with Soren.

Pacing the bedroom, I try to focus on getting my shit together, but I'm not making much progress.

There's a knock on the bedroom door a few minutes later. "How're you doing?" Soren asks, his voice muffled by the door between us.

"I...I'm not feeling well..." I don't know if Adrien's with him or not, and I don't think either of us is prepared to explain to him what's really going on right now. That's a conversation that can wait until he's a bit older...if I'm still around, that is.

"Do you need some soup?" Adrien asks through the door. "My dad made me soup one time when I was sick."

"Thank you, but I think I just need to lie down..."

He's such a sweet kid. He doesn't deserve all the crap he's had to go through. "Oh...okay." Adrien sounds a little disappointed.

"I think it's time for some stories," Soren says with a reassuring tone. "Let's let Luke get some rest."

"Get some rest, Luke," Adrien calls to me.

"I will, thank you." I do my best to sound cheerful, but it's difficult. My cheeks are burning with embarrassment, and my body is trembling with need as my hormones beg me to jump that sexy alpha and ride his knot until this passes.

I sink to the floor beside Soren's bed and listen to the sound of footsteps withdrawing from the door.

My condition has brought me endless misery over the course of my life. Holding down normal jobs has been impossible, and getting long-term clients through Omega for Hire hasn't really worked out for me either. I even had to drop out of high school in my freshman year when we first learned about my condition.

My grandmother homeschooled me and made sure I had a safe place to hide when I went into heat each month. And she tried to get me help. She took me to doctors and specialists all over the country, but there was nothing anyone could do for me. Apparently, my condition is so rare that only a handful of omegas in the world have to deal with it.

Talk about the wrong lottery to win.

Everyone else just pops a suppressant each day and goes about their life as normal. Meanwhile, I live in fear of what's to come each month. And it's completely unpredictable. I never know when it will strike, so planning ahead isn't an option. Spending a lot of time in very close proximity to an alpha might be a trigger, but it's an inconsistent one.

Not sure what else to do, I stretch out on the floor and stare up at the ceiling, ignoring my erection. There's no point in trying to masturbate right now. I'll just be horny again in a few minutes. There will be no relief until this is over. Not to mention that my ass is starting to throb with need.

It's already slick in anticipation of an alpha's cock.

And on the other side of that door, just down the hall from me, is an alpha. One who is broad-shouldered, muscular, and tall. I'm sure his cock is just as impressive as he is. It wouldn't take much for him to satisfy this empty feeling that's driving me wild. His knot would put an end to all of our misery.

My chest heaves as I pant for breath. The racing of my heart is making it hard for me to think straight. Before I know it, I'm stroking my dick and biting my lip to keep from making any noise that might give me away.

It's impossible to resist seeking relief when every single inch of your body wants the same thing.

I don't know how much time passes before there's a knock on the door. I freeze mid stroke, precome running down my shaft and over my fingers. The floor below me is soaked with slick, and a sheen of sweat coats my body.

"Luke?" Soren's voice is quiet but still audible.

I swallow hard and try to get my breathing under control. "Y-yes?"

"Adrien's asleep." He pauses for a moment and then clears his throat. "If you want, I can help."

I nearly choke on my heart as it leaps into my throat. I scramble to my knees and clutch my hands into white-knuckled fists, trying to stop them from yanking the door open. "But...I don't want to ruin things..." It sounds like a terrible excuse as I sit there, stinking to high heaven. "I like taking care of you...both of you. I don't want to lose what we have."

"This doesn't have to mean anything," Soren says. "We don't have to complicate this. But...I checked the news. There are trees down all over the place. The schools are closed, and a lot of places are out of power. We're going to be stuck here for a while. And you're going to be stuck in there...and I can already smell you."

Why does my stupid body have to ruin everything. I'm nothing but a plague to the people around me. "I'm so sorry, Soren."

"My point is that you can't stay locked up in there the whole time." Soren's voice is stronger now, more confident. "So, let me help. I promise, this won't change anything. You mean too much to us for it to change things."

My breathing is ragged as I slowly climb to my feet. The anticipation is killing me. Just knowing there's a willing alpha within reach has doubled the neediness permeating my body. "Are you sure?"

"I'm positive. Just tell me what you need. I want to help."

14

—

SOREN

THE DOOR UNLOCKS with an audible click, and I reach for the knob.

I'd caught Luke's scent as soon as I stepped into the hallway after putting Adrien to bed. Despite our long afternoon nap, he's already fast asleep. Though it did take several books to get there.

Apparently, that was just long enough for Luke's scent to radiate through the rest of the apartment and hit me like a brick wall when I stepped into it.

My throat is dry as I slowly push the door open. The sight that greets me sends a shiver down my spine and straight through to my aching dick.

Luke's dressed only in one of my t-shirts. His erect

cock is peeking out from beneath the shirt, and I can see precome glistening in the light as he stands there, waiting for me.

"Luke…" I breathe out his name as I step into the room. His scent is stronger here. So strong that my desire for him instantly doubles.

No more words. No more restraint. I need to let loose and give him the ride of a lifetime.

Somehow, I manage to stay rooted in place.

"Soren…" Luke chews his lip, clearly overcome with the same desperation that's coursing through me. "Promise that this won't change anything. I can't…can't let it change anything."

"It won't." My breathing rasps against my throat. "Just tell me what I can do to help you."

"Fuck…" Luke's eyes are glassy as he reaches for me. "Me…"

I'm not sure I'm even going to last long enough to sate his heat with the way I'm feeling. "Luke…"

"Fuck…me…" He repeats a little more urgently. "Please, Soren."

I step farther into the room, ready to do just that.

"Fuck me...Soren." Luke grabs his cock and strokes it a few times.

With the bedroom door locked behind me, there are no more reasons to wait. I pull my shirt off, unable to hold myself back any longer.

"Yes, please..." Luke breathes heavily as I stride toward him.

As soon as I'm within reach, I pull him into my arms and find his delicious mouth eagerly awaiting mine. His tongue slides against mine as his free hand slips down the front of my pajama pants and grabs my cock.

His heated skin feels like heaven as he strokes my shaft.

Without pulling away, I shed my pants and kick them aside, freeing myself of the last of my clothing. "Now you." My breath bounces against his lips as I make just enough room between us to tug the shirt that's barely concealing his form over his head.

He gasps as soon as he's completely exposed to me. "Fuck..."

With a growl of desire, I lift him into my arms and carry him the last few feet to the bed.

Luke sucks greedily on my neck and shoulder the entire time, leaving a mark that's sure to become a hickey later. "Soren..."

The way he says my name sends a wave of constant shivers through my cock.

"I need you inside me..." His eyes are begging as much as his mouth is.

"And I need to fuck you." I crawl onto the bed beside him then slide between his legs. "Do you see how hard you've made me?"

Luke looks down at my cock, and his eyes grow wide. "Oh, fuck. You're huge."

He's not the first omega to tell me that, but it means more coming from him. Instead of just boosting my ego, I feel both pride and concern over how I might hurt him. "Are you ready for me?"

"More than." He curls his legs behind my back and draws me closer. "Fill me with that massive cock. I can take it all."

I don't have the patience to go through the steps of checking for myself. My dick is hard, his ass is ready, it's time to fuck.

The head of my cock slides easily into his slick-soaked hole. Any doubts I had about his ability to take all of me are instantly dispelled. Pressing forward, I moan as his ass envelopes me perfectly, pulling me in and massaging my cock like it was made for me.

"Yesssssss…" Luke breathes once the last few inches of my dick disappear inside him. "That's perfect. Oh, fuck… Soren!"

I reach forward and give his cock a few tugs as he clutches the blankets on either side of him.

"Oh…fuck…" He moans again, arching his back off the bed and pulling me even deeper with his legs around my thighs. "I want…fuck…fuck me…Soren, fuck me…"

His needy begging is more than I can take. I plant my hands on either side of him and begin to move in a steady tempo. My hips meet his thighs with a soft slap of bare skin. Slowly, my pace builds, and his ass squeezes my dick with every motion.

Luke bites his lip, desperate to keep his voice low, despite the sloppy sounds of sex filling the air around us.

My balls are tight, filled to bursting with come. Every instinct I have is telling me to release inside him. To give him the knot I can already feel beginning to form.

He meets my gaze as if sensing the question on the tip of my tongue. "Don't you dare pull out." His eyes are wild as he looks up at me. "I need it, Soren. I need your knot."

The lust in his words and the look in his eyes are all the encouragement I need to continue.

I drive forward, my cock slamming home one final time and exploding within him as my knot seals the gap and locks in my come. Caught up in the moment, I press my lips to his as my come continues to shoot into him.

Luke curls his arms around my shoulders and shudders beneath me as he comes too. Hot cream splashes against my chest as our kiss continues. His mouth is sweet, his lips soft, and his tongue greedy. I can't remember the last time I had a kiss this fulfilling.

As we finally pull apart, our eyes meet, and my heart thrums against my ribs as I try to catch my breath. Looking into his eyes, I'm instantly aware of an inescapable truth.

There's no going back from this. Despite what I promised, everything's going to be different from now on.

15

———

LUKE

"I'm sorry…" I look around the room at the mess that we've made. "I kind of ruined some things."

Soren is digging through his dresser for some clean pajamas while I sit on the edge of the bed. "You didn't ruin anything," he assures me as he hands me a clean t-shirt. "Do you feel better now?"

"Yeah, but—"

"Then it was worth it." He winks, teasing me. "More than worth it. It's not like I didn't enjoy myself too."

"Yes…but…" I take a deep breath and look down at the shirt in my hands. "We can't pretend that this doesn't change things at all. Can we?"

Soren falls silent for a minute, just staring at the drawer of clothing. "We could. If that's what you want. It doesn't have to mean anything."

"What do you want?" I can sense the hesitation in his words as I pull the shirt over my head and create at least a thin barrier between our naked bodies. "Do you want it to mean something?"

Soren doesn't turn back to me as he begins to dress himself. "You're the one who decides. I...I can pretend it didn't mean anything, if that's what you want."

There's a tinge of pain in his voice as he speaks. He doesn't want to pretend, but he made a promise that nothing would change. He's torn between what he wants and what he promised.

"Every relationship I've ever had has ended in flames." I sigh and look down at my feet. "Despite everything I feel right now...I'm scared that will happen again."

"You're not the only one who's got a shitty track record with relationships." Dressed, he finally turns around and looks at me. "Just...answer one question. What exactly are you feeling right now?"

I bite my lip so hard it hurts as I try to put my feelings into words. "I feel...like I don't want this to end." It takes a moment but I want to be honest with him. I owe him that much. "I feel like...I want to be kissed like that again and again. I want to wake up with you beside me every morning. I want..." I press my hand against my stomach and close my eyes to keep in the tears I'm afraid might form. "I want to be pregnant with your baby."

I feel Soren's gaze on me from across the room, but he's not speaking, and that makes me worried. I can't bring myself to look up at him, though. I'm afraid that the moment I do, this wonderful evening will turn into a nightmare.

"Luke..." Soren's voice is surprisingly calm when he starts speaking. "If you don't want this to end, then—"

The lights flicker, and then we're immediately plunged into darkness. Eerie silence fills the air as we remain motionless in the pitch-black room. Within seconds, the first tendrils of cold air slowly replace the warmth that was flowing through the vents.

"Something must've brought down a power line,"

Soren says after a minute. "Do you know where your phone is? I can't find mine."

"Hang on." I scoot along the edge of the bed until I find the spot where I dropped my pants earlier. My phone is still tucked inside the pocket. A few quick swipes later, and the flashlight glows to life. I pan the light across the room until Soren locates his phone and can turn its light on too.

"I've got some candles and flashlights in the kitchen." His gaze lands on me, and he purses his lips. "We're probably going to need some extra blankets, and you're going to want to put some pants on. It'll get cold in here soon."

"Right." I grab the pajama bottoms he set out for me earlier and pull them on. "Just tell me what to do. I can help now."

Soren is already opening the bedroom door and glancing down the hallway. "In my closet are some extra blankets." He nods toward the closet on the far side of the room. "You should try to clean things up as best you can and then layer a few more blankets on the bed. I'm gonna grab a few candles and then get Adrien. If he wakes up alone in the dark..." His voice trails off and he shakes his head. "I don't want him to get scared. His room is going to get cold without heat too."

"I understand." With a quick nod, I head to the closet. "I'll get everything ready in here."

Soren disappears into the darkness, and I quickly set to work. I strip the top blanket off the bed and toss it in the corner with the rest of our dirty clothes. With those out of the way, I use my dirty t-shirt to clean up as much of the mess on the floor as I can. It's not perfect, but it'll do for now.

I'm in the middle of layering the extra blankets on the bed when Soren returns with a couple candles and some matches.

"Took me longer to find these than I thought." He carefully balances the various assortment in his arms. "It's been eons since I've needed them."

"I got it." I take his load and set it all on the dresser. "Go get Adrien."

He shoots me a grateful nod and presses a quick kiss to my forehead before darting out into the darkness once more.

I stand in stunned silence for a moment. Was that just gratitude? Or was it more than that? What was he going to say before we were interrupted? There are so many questions I need answers to, but I don't have time to dwell on them right now. I've got things to do. My internal emotional turmoil will have to wait.

Selecting the biggest candle, I light it and place it in the center of the dresser so there's no chance the flame will catch on anything else. The soft, orange glow flickers to life and chases away most of the shadows. I decide to leave the other candles unlit for now. There's enough light in the room to finish making the bed without the aid of my cell phone. I should conserve that battery since we could be out of power for days.

Just as I finish layering the last blanket on the bed, Soren returns with a sleepy Adrien in his arms.

"See, it's a sleepover. Just like you wanted." Soren glances at me, nodding to the bed.

I pull back the covers, and he puts Adrien down in the middle of the bed.

"Are you feeling better?" Adrien asks when he sees me.

"Yes." I give him a little smile. "I'm much better now."

"That's good." Adrien yawns then lies back against the pillows. "This will be the best sleepover ever."

"I felt bad waking him up, but the rest of the house is already getting cold, so I didn't want to risk it." Soren circles around the bed to the other side.

"Probably the right call." I climb into bed next to Adrien and pull the covers up over us.

He's already starting to drift off again.

Soren climbs into bed, and soon, the three of us are nice and toasty beneath our blankets.

I stare up at the ceiling overhead, watching the candlelight flicker. The suddenness of the power outage chased all thoughts of sleep from my head, but now that we're all tucked in, exhaustion washes over me.

Just as sleep closes in, I hear Soren's soft voice. It's quiet, whispered, but clear. "Sleep well. I love you both."

16

SOREN

"WAKE UP!" Adrien shouts, bouncing in the middle of the bed.

My eyes snap open, adrenaline surging through my veins. One thought rings clear in my mind. I have to protect my family.

"Wake up, wake up, wake up," Adrien continues in a sing-song chant as he jumps up and down on the mattress.

It takes me a minute to realize that nothing's actually wrong, and he's just goofing off.

"How do you have so much energy so early in the morning?" I slowly sit up, trying to will my eyes to stay open. When they do, my gaze lands on the far side of the bed where Luke should be. I'm more than a little disappointed to see that he's gone. The candle on the dresser has been put out too, and daylight streams in through the blinds over the window.

"Luke said to ask if you want breakfast." Adrien drops into a squat on the bed. "He says you're a sleepyhead."

Adrien is grinning from ear to ear. It's good to see him in such a good mood. I'm still getting used to him talking to me so freely, but he doesn't seem bothered at all in my presence.

"Maybe you two just have too much energy." I playfully throw back the covers and slowly crawl out of bed. The chill in the air is even more pronounced than it was last night. I guess that explains why Adrien's wearing a sweater over his PJs.

"Luke says the power died last night." Adrien ignores my comment and continues on with his myriad of questions. "Why did it die?"

My back is a little tight, but other than that, I feel amazing. "I don't know for sure. But the storm last night probably caused it."

Adrien frowns as he shuffles off the bed. "But that means we have no lights, and the TV doesn't turn on. Luke says we can't cook food either."

"For now." I go in search of some socks and slippers. There's no way I'm going barefoot in this cold. "But I'm sure they've got people fixing it right now."

"When will it be fixed?" Adrien is at my side, talking to me just as comfortably as he does with Luke.

"I don't really know." I pull on my socks then step into my slippers. "But until it is, we'll just have to sit tight and wait."

"Oh…" Adrien tilts his head thoughtfully. I'm not sure he fully understands what I'm saying, but he's definitely trying. "Do you have to go to work today?"

I purse my lips as I reach for my phone. "That's a very good question, actually. I'll have to call my boss and find out."

Adrien seems pleased with my response. "Tell him you can't work today because you have to stay with me and Luke."

I smile softly. Hearing that he wants me to stay fills my heart with warmth. He might not be ready to call me "Dad" yet, but this gives me hope that maybe one day, he will.

"Come on." I head toward the door and gesture for him to follow. "Let's go see what Luke's up to."

"He's making breakfast, I told you." Adrien rolls his eyes and runs out the door ahead of me. Nice to see that his spirits aren't dampened by the sudden change in circumstances.

As I emerge from the hallway, Luke is in the kitchen putting together sandwiches from last night's leftovers. When he sees me, he smiles, and my heart melts.

I don't think he heard the words I whispered into the stillness last night. The verbal confession of everything that's in my heart right now. I'm not sure I'm ready to tell him to his face either. I don't want to push things to move too fast. Really, our situation is tenuous, at best.

When Luke told me how he felt, he caught me off guard, and there are a lot of questions I still don't know how to answer completely.

Until I figure that out, I can't honestly describe how I feel.

"How'd you sleep?" Luke asks as I follow Adrien over to the dining table.

"Like a rock." I stifle a yawn. If I'm being perfectly honest, I'd probably still be asleep if it wasn't for Adrien's wake-up call. "You?"

"It was nice and warm under the covers," he says wistfully. "I didn't want to get up, but once the sun came up, I couldn't go back to sleep."

Adrien is busily painting a watercolor page and doesn't bother looking at either of us.

"He got up about half an hour ago and asked if he could paint." Luke's eyes are on Adrien too. "He's been hard at work ever since."

I try to get a glimpse of what he's working on, but Adrien hides it with his arms.

His little brows furrow as he looks up at me with a frown. "You can see it when it's finished."

"Yeah, you can't look at it yet," Luke says with a light laugh. "I got scolded already for trying to peek earlier."

"Oh, sorry." I smile apologetically and back away a few steps, "I didn't realize it was a secret."

Adrien watches me guardedly for a moment and then goes back to work.

"I'll have these done in a minute." Luke gestures to the plates in front of him. "I know it's not much, but we can't really cook anything right now."

"It looks fantastic." I wink in reassurance and then pull out my cell phone. I've got a few missed calls from my boss. "I'm going to make a quick phone call, and then I'll be right back."

Luke nods silently and watches me depart. He doesn't have to say anything for me to know that he's worried I'm going to attempt to go to the office. His expression says it all.

I drop onto the sofa in the living room and stare at the log of missed calls with growing dread. Something tells me I'm going to regret making this call. Of course, I could just pretend my phone died last night, and I wasn't able to answer right away.

But that's not who I am.

I take a deep breath and make the call. Ignoring a problem that's staring me in the face isn't my style. I have to do something about it, even if that something is just telling them that I'm not available.

"Soren, it's about damn time." Robert's voice roars to life. "I've been trying to get a hold of you all morning."

"I had my phone off to conserve the battery," I explain calmly. "I don't have a way to charge it with the power out."

"Fine, whatever, just get to the office as soon as you can." Robert sounds exasperated. "With the power outage last night, alarm systems are down all over the city. There were dozens of break-ins, and now we've got a backlog of claims being filed from some of our biggest accounts. I need you here to reassure these people. Let them know we've got things under control. Otherwise, they're going to start pulling out of their contracts."

As Robert rants, I'm vaguely aware of Luke approaching me from the kitchen. I meet his gaze, and he nods to his phone as he hands it to me.

Confused, I frown but glance at the screen. There's a news article with a prominent headline urging people to stay off the streets. Icy roads, as well as downed trees and power lines, have created dangerous conditions.

"Wait, wait, wait." I nod a thank-you to Luke as I quickly cut Robert off. "Have you taken a look outside? They're telling people to stay off the roads."

"Which means you won't have to worry about traffic." Robert's in a shitty mood, and apparently, I get to be his sounding board. "Soren, you're the only one who can do this. Our clients know you're a man of your word."

"They also know the streets aren't safe right now. They can't honestly expect you to have people in the office today." I hand Luke back his phone as I try to reason with my boss.

"I've already got people in the office." Robert doesn't seem concerned about his employees at all. "But those idiots don't know what they're doing without guidance. You need to get down there, Soren. Your job depends on it."

I sit straight up at those words. Did he really just threaten my job? All because I don't want to risk the roads right now? "You can't be serious." I rise from the sofa and begin to pace. "You're asking me to put my life, and the lives of others, at risk because you don't have the balls to tell your clients the office is closed today."

"Excuse me?" Robert's tone is deadly calm, and it's only now that I fully realize what I said to him. What's even more surprising is that I don't regret it in the slightest.

"I have to think about what's best for my family." I briefly glance at Adrien and Luke. "That means not going out and risking my life over something trivial. The power's out all over the city. I doubt the office has power. Which means the entire computer system is offline. There's no way to get anything done right now anyway."

"Soren, I'm going to urge you to take a moment and think about what you just said." Robert sounds like he's on the verge of yelling, and it's only through sheer force of will that he hasn't yet.

"I don't need to think about it," I assure him. "You could have been reasonable and asked me to make phone calls from home, or maybe reach out to our clients through email. You could have told our clients that we're all in the same boat right now, and you're not willing to risk your employees' safety. But instead, you decided to threaten me."

"It wasn't a threat, Soren. It was a promise." Robert takes a deep breath. "You can forget about the promotion we were discussing. If you're not in the office by ten, then don't bother ever coming back."

With that, the line goes dead.

I exhale forcefully and lower my head as I stare at the blank screen of my phone. I've known Robert for years now. He's a workaholic and a bit of a jerk when he's under pressure, but I've never considered him unreasonable before. Thinking back on the past several years, I'm starting to wonder if maybe I was just blind.

Work was my whole life before. But now…

"Is everything okay?" Luke's voice is timid, unsure.

I put my cell phone on the coffee table and start laughing. "I think I just lost my job."

Luke's eyes are wide with surprise. "You're...laughing about that?"

"Yeah, I guess I am." I pause for a moment before chuckling again. "He threatened to fire me if I didn't come in to work. And...I basically told him to go fuck himself."

"Soren, language!" Luke nods toward Adrien who is watching me intently.

My cheeks flush, and I quickly apologize. "Sorry, yes. I shouldn't have said that. But it wasn't that long ago that I would've been one of those people risking everything to get to the office right now. Nothing mattered to me more than my career." I smile softly as I look at Adrien and then Luke. "Now, I've got other priorities."

"You're not going to work today?" Adrien slides off his chair and stands up.

"No, I'm not."

Without warning, he darts across the living room and flings himself into my arms.

I wrap him up in a big hug and give him a squeeze.

"Now you can play with me and Luke some more," Adrien says as he wiggles out of my arms. "We can do puzzles, and paint, and play games, and..." He frowns and ponders other things to add to his list.

"And eat breakfast," Luke fills in the first item on the list. "Come sit down and eat, Adrien."

Adrien points at Luke as he approaches the table. "Don't look at my painting!" He springs across the room and scrambles into his chair to protect his artwork from the eyes of others.

"I'm not looking, I swear." Luke uses his palm to shield his eyes before setting a plate down next to Adrien. "But you need to put it somewhere safe for now so you can eat."

He looks up at Luke. "In my room?"

"Yeah, put it on your dresser for now. You can work on it more later." Luke nods and reaches for the cup of blueish water. "I'll clean up the paints, okay?"

Adrien grabs his painting and runs off to store it somewhere safe.

Taking my cue, I jump up from the sofa. "I'll clean up the paints, Luke. You've been busy all morning, and I haven't done anything."

Luke forces a smile and looks at me with concern in his eyes. "Are you sure you're okay?"

"Yeah, I'm fine." I grin, genuinely feeling happier than I can remember. "Why wouldn't I be? I just made a life-changing decision to throw away a career that's consumed the last ten years of my life."

"I'm being serious, Soren." Luke leans against the kitchen counter as I gather up the rest of the painting supplies. "This is kind of a big deal. Don't take this the wrong way, but your career seems to be a big part of your identity."

I cock my head, surprised by his reaction. "Do you think I made the wrong decision?"

"No, I just...I want to make sure you're not having an identity crisis or something." Luke forces a smile. "You're important to me. To us."

"Exactly." I blow out a long breath and smile. "That's why I'm doing this. Because...this job, it's not who I am anymore. I think I've been coming to terms with it all week, but I didn't fully realize it until yesterday. Adrien is the most important thing in the world to me now. There's no way I can go out there and risk my life on those icy roads, because if something happens to me, then what happens to him?"

I pause to think about my next words as I put the paints on the counter. "If I were to die right now, what happens to him?" I look back at Luke. "My ex is up and gone, so Adrien would go into the system. And even though I know you care about him, unless you could get approved for adoption, there's nothing you could do to prevent it."

Luke's eyes soften, his expression filled with pain.

"I'm not saying this to upset you." I reach for his hand and hold it. "I just want you to understand. I'm willing to sacrifice everything to make sure that doesn't happen. Because I never want Adrien to be alone again."

Luke opens his mouth to speak, but he closes it up as soon as Adrien marches out into the living room again. "I hid it so you guys can't go snooping." Adrien climbs up into his chair again. "You can see it when it's done, so don't look under my bed."

"Okay, I promise I won't," I assure him.

"Me too," Luke agrees. "Now, let's eat."

17

———

LUKE

THINGS ARE…CONFUSING, to say the least. Or maybe I'm the only one who's confused.

As I sit on the sofa and cradle a mug of hot cocoa, I watch Adrien's sleeping face. He's snuggled down in a nest of blankets and pillows that looks downright cozy.

The temperature outside has warmed up enough for the ice to melt, but it's still raining hard and the wind is blowing. According to the news updates on my phone, there are still power lines and trees down all over the place. They're still urging people to stay home unless it's an absolute emergency. Needless to say, the power is out for the foreseeable future, and the power company has no idea when it'll be back.

"Thank you for your patience." Soren is on the other side of the room, pacing comfortably in front of the window as he talks into his cell phone. "I understand completely how frustrating this situation is… Absolutely. I agree completely. The safety of your employees should be a top priority."

He's been making phone calls for the last half-hour after getting a sudden flash of inspiration. I don't understand completely, but in the span of an hour, he went from being unemployed to making business phone calls.

I wish my grief and confusion could be overcome with a few phone calls.

Unfortunately, it's all an internal struggle that I'm not sure how to resolve. Now that I have time to sit and think to myself, I keep going over the events from last night. Neither of us has really said anything more about it.

Soren's certainly acting differently. He keeps saying stuff like "my family," and the way he glances at me when he says it makes me think he's not just referring to Adrien. But he hasn't given any context to it. I'm starting to wonder if I imagined the words he said before I fell asleep last night. Maybe it was just wishful thinking caused by all the hormones and emotions running through me.

I dumped a lot of shit on him last night when I confessed how I was feeling. The fact that he still hasn't given me a proper answer makes me wonder if I should've kept it to myself. Maybe played things cool after we had sex. It could've just been something casual. He helped me with a problem and that was it. If I was lucky, maybe he'd agree to help me every month. Having a standing monthly hookup with Soren sounded like a pretty good perk of working for him.

Instead, I dumped all my pent-up emotions on him and told him exactly what I was feeling at the time.

"I did it." Soren pockets his phone and returns to the sofa with a triumphant gleam in his eye.

"Did what?" I'd rather not come across as an emotional mess, even if that's what I'm quickly turning into.

"Okay, so..." Soren picks up his hot chocolate mug from the coffee table and turns to face me. "I just managed to secure the three biggest accounts from my old job. These people only signed on with the company because of the relationship I cultivated with them. All I had to do was tell them that I was being forced to leave the company, and I'm striking out on my own. The rest took care of itself."

My jaw drops open in shock. "You're starting your own business?"

Soren nods. "After thinking about it for most of the morning, I realized I could handle the majority of the work right here from home. We already contract out a bunch of stuff, so I have contacts throughout the industry. The framework is already there. All I really needed was a few loyal clients with deep pockets, and I can secure a steady income without the crippling workload I had before."

"That's...great." I'm stunned by the speed at which he's changed gears.

"There's still a bit of legwork left to do, but the hard part is out of the way. I can handle a lot of the high-level stuff with a few phone calls and emails. Really, the majority of the job is just delegation." He's looking out the window at the sheets of rain still falling. "The only reason I was working such crazy hours was the sheer number of contracts we were managing all the time. But I don't have to pay hundreds of employees or cover the costs associated with a massive firm. I just need enough for the three of us."

"Soren..." I bite my lip and stare down into my clasped hands.

"What's wrong?" He reaches across the sofa and places a hand on my knee. "Did I do something wrong?"

"I'm just trying to figure out what all this means." I shake my head slowly but don't look up at him. "I don't understand where I fit into all this. I mean...I know what I want...but I don't know what you want. Am I the babysitter or..." I finally lift my eyes to look at him as I ask the question that's been eating away at me. "What am I to you?"

"I've been trying to put everything into words all morning." His expression softens, and he sets his cup aside before sliding closer to me. "And every time I come close, I find myself second-guessing everything. All this is happening so fast that I'm afraid if I stop to think, then I'll realize I was making it all up and there was nothing there to begin with."

I swallow hard, afraid he's going to say he just wants me to be the babysitter for now...or forever.

He gently presses his forehead to mine and exhales slowly. "You were more open with me than I was expecting last night. It wasn't that long ago that I'd never even thought about having a family. Now, I've got Adrien, and you were talking about having a baby. Until last night, babies were one of the furthest things from my mind."

"I'm sorry. I know it was kind of a crazy thing to unload on you." I glance at him and try to laugh off the weight of the topic. "You asked me what I wanted, and I just blurted it all out without thinking about the consequences. I like kids, that's why I'm a babysitter, but having my own is just something I thought would happen someday in the future. Honestly, it was kinda out of the blue for me too."

"This last week has been one of the best of my life." He kisses my forehead and sits back slightly so he can look me in the eye. "Getting to know you and Adrien has been more fulfilling than I ever could've imagined. And yesterday, for the first time in ages, I actually felt like I had a family with me. Last night, as I held you in my arms, I realized I never wanted to let you go. You caught me off guard with your candid confessions, but I was more than happy to hear them."

Soren grabs my hands and tugs me into his warm, reassuring embrace. "I want to be your alpha, Luke," he says once I'm safely enveloped in his arms. "I want to keep you safe, to provide for your needs, and make sure you always feel loved."

I bury my face against his neck and inhale his scent. He tilts his head toward me and meets my lips in a warm, deep kiss. His love and adoration are evident in that kiss, free of the haze of lust that shrouded us last night. In my heart, I know this is where I'm meant to be.

"Gross!" Adrien's squeal catches us by surprise, and we quickly break the kiss to look over at him. He's sitting up among his blankets and frowning at us. "Do you guys have to be that gross? I'm trying to sleep here."

18

———

SOREN

THE POWER IS off for the rest of the day, but we get by with lots of layers and heavy blankets. Thankfully, the small camping stove still had fuel I was able to use to heat water for instant cocoa. That was a life-saver when Adrien began to melt down over not being able to turn on the TV.

When the sun starts to set, we all sit in the living room and put together puzzles by candlelight.

Adrien quickly got over his disgust at catching me and Luke kissing. Though not before declaring there was no way he was ever going to kiss someone because it was just too icky.

"Okay, so...I think we definitely need to invest in some new puzzles," Luke says as we finish our current project. "How many times have we done this one now?"

Adrien throws out a number. "Umm...ten?"

I chuckle. "I think it's closer to three."

"It feels like ten." Adrien groans and leans away from the table. "Why does the power have to be dead?"

"It just happens sometimes." Luke shrugs and glances out the window at the darkening sky. "We've just got to hold out till it comes back."

"But when will it come back?"

We've had this conversation, or one like it, at least a dozen times today. Adrien's not the only one going a little stir-crazy either. I've been fighting the urge to check my phone in an effort to conserve the battery. I'm sure Luke's struggling with the same thing. If this power outage lasts much longer, we'll have to get really creative with our entertainment options.

"It's a mystery." Luke rises from the floor and heads to the kitchen to figure out dinner. "But if it doesn't come back soon, we're going to start losing things in the refrigerator."

I swear under my breath. I just went shopping two days ago, so the refrigerator is pretty much full of fresh food. We've been limiting our access to the fridge to keep it as cool as possible, but there's only so much we can do.

Eventually stuff will start going bad.

Adrien tightens the blanket around his shoulders and looks across the table at me with a deeply furrowed brow.

"What's that look for?" I quirk an eyebrow.

"Yesterday, you said Luke was a friend." Adrien folds his hands and rests them on the coffee table.

"Yes...I did say that." I nod in agreement.

"But today, you were kissing him." Adrien cocks his head as if concentrating on the situation. "You're not supposed to kiss friends."

I purse my lips, not sure how to respond to that. "Well, I guess Luke's not just a friend anymore."

Adrien's eyes go wide and he looks suddenly happy. "So you love him?"

I look toward Luke. He's busy in the kitchen, and I don't think he can hear our conversation.

"Yeah." I look back at Adrien as I admit the words that seem crazy to my own ears but are truer than any I've ever spoken before. "I do love Luke."

"You said love means that someone is your family." Adrien looks at Luke and then back at me. "Is Luke your family now?"

I smile softly. "Yeah, he is. Luke is part of my family. Just like you are."

Adrien's eyes drop down for a moment, and he doesn't say anything.

Did I say too much? His therapist warned me not to push him too hard.

After a moment of silence, Adrien stands up and heads to his bedroom without another word.

Luke pauses in the middle of cooking and tilts his head as he watches Adrien walk past.

"What's that about?" Luke asks, meeting my gaze.

"I don't know." I climb to my feet and join Luke in the kitchen. "He was asking me all these questions about if I love you and if you are our family. So I told him you are our family just like he is. And then..." I gesture toward the hallway. "Do you think I went too far?"

"I don't think so." Luke frowns and shakes his head. "Let's just see what he does first. If he doesn't come back on his own, then I'll check on him in a few minutes."

"Are you sure?" I hate the thought that I might have done something to mess up all the progress we've made over the past few days. We can't go back to the way things were when Adrien first came home.

Before Luke can reply, Adrien emerges from the hallway with a piece of paper clutched in his hands. "It's so cold in my room." He marches toward us and doesn't look like he's relapsing.

"What'cha got there?" Luke asks him.

"It's my painting." Adrien looks down at the paper for a long minute. "I made it for you guys."

Despite his words, he doesn't make any move to hand it over.

"Really?" Luke flashes a broad grin. "Why don't we all go sit on the sofa and you can show it to us?"

Adrien falls into step behind Luke, shadowing him all the way into the living room. We sit down with Adrien between us, but he keeps the painting clutched to his chest. As much as he wants to share it with us, something seems to be holding him back.

"I'd love to see your painting, Adrien," Luke says gently. "Wouldn't you, Soren?"

I nod and place my hand on his back. "Absolutely. You've been working on it all morning, so I can't wait to see."

"Just...promise you won't tear it up," Adrien says after a moment.

"Promise," Luke says without hesitation. "I'd never do that."

"Same," I quickly chime in. "I promise." Now I'm curious to see if this is yet another thing I have to thank my ex for.

Adrien takes a deep breath and presents his painting with a flourish. He's taken a blank piece of paper and created a lovely stick-figure scene featuring three people. There are flowers and a sun and something that might be a swingset.

"Oh, Adrien, this is beautiful," Luke gushes excitedly. "Is this you?" He points to the short stick figure in the middle of the two bigger ones.

Adrien nods slowly. "That's me, and this is you..." He points to the slightly taller stick figure. "And...this is Dad." He points to the biggest stick figure before looking up at me. "That's you."

My vision blurs, and my throat suddenly feels tight. "You made me so big and strong," I say as I try to get my emotions under control. "I really like it."

"I painted the three of us together because we're a family." Adrien looks back down at the paper and swings his legs animatedly. "We're outside on a sunny day, and we're at the park together."

"Is that something you want to do?" My hand inches up to his shoulder and I give him a tentative squeeze. "When the sun comes out again?"

"Yeah...I want all three of us to go to the park." Adrien smiles down at his paper. "Do you guys really like it?"

"I think it's wonderful," I assure him.

"It's beautiful," Luke agrees. "In fact...can I hold it? I promise to be careful."

Adrien looks at his painting and then relinquishes it to Luke. "Be careful, I worked hard."

"I know you did," Luke says with a smile. "Artwork like this deserves to be displayed somewhere safe so we can see it all the time."

"Like where?" Adrien seems excited by the idea.

"The refrigerator door?" I suggest, knowing exactly what Luke is suggesting.

"Exactly!" Luke stands and marches over to the refrigerator with Adrien close behind. He grabs a magnet from the door and hangs it prominently in the middle. "What do you think, Adrien?"

"Maybe...a little that way?" Adrien points to the left.

Luke adjusts it. "This way?"

"Yeah, there."

I rise from the sofa and join them in the kitchen.

"Perfect." I kneel beside Adrien as we look up at the painting. "You're a real artist."

Adrien is silent for a very long moment. "My dad...my other dad...said I couldn't be a painter because painters don't make any money."

I cock an eyebrow. "Do you like painting?"

Adrien nods.

"Then you can be a painter. You can be anything you want to be, Adrien." I give him another small squeeze, and he responds by throwing his arms around my neck and crying. His tiny body shakes with every sob as he pours out all the emotions he's been keeping pent up for who knows how long.

Luke kneels beside us, and I wrap an arm around him too.

"Are we really a family?" Adrien asks, sniffling softly as he leans back to look at both of us.

"You, and me, and Luke." I nod and sniffle back some of my own emotions. "We're really a family."

"Always?"

"Always." Luke places his head on my shoulder.

And right then, the lights flicker back on.

LUKE

WITH THE POWER BACK, I'm able to prepare an actual hot meal for everyone. By the time we're done eating, the temperature in the apartment has returned to normal and we're all peeling out of the extra layers of clothing we've been wearing.

Adrien passes out on the living room floor not long after we finish eating. He's had a big day, and it's no surprise that he's exhausted.

Soren scoops him up and carries him to his bed while I finish cleaning up after dinner.

Every time I pass the refrigerator, I get a small spring in my step. Adrien's painting puts a smile on my face and lightens my heart. I'm not just part of Soren's family. I belong to Adrien as well. Together, the three of us are a family.

A family I'd never dared to hope I would be a part of.

"I'm sorry for breaking my promise," Soren says as he returns to the kitchen.

"Which promise?" I place the last of the leftovers in the fridge and close the door.

He responds by taking my hands and sweeping me into his arms. "Last night, I promised that nothing would change. That no matter what happened in the heat of the moment, things would stay the same. But less than a day later, nothing is the same anymore."

"Do you regret it at all?" I ask, though I'm confident I already know the answer.

"Not in the least. It turns out that you're the missing piece." He looks into my eyes and gently caresses my cheek. "I've spent my whole life trying to find purpose. I thought I'd find it through my career if I could just climb high enough. Then Adrien arrived, and I started to doubt everything I ever knew. But it wasn't until last night that I realized my true purpose in life."

I shiver beneath his touches and loop my arms around his neck. For the first time in my life, I don't question that this is where I belong. I'm not worried that I'll be sent packing or told someone better has been found. "And what's that?"

"To be your alpha." He says it as if it's the most obvious thing in the world. "To raise a family with you."

"That makes me happier than you'll ever know." I kiss him gently on the lips and then again along his jaw and neck. "All I want is to be your omega. When I said I never wanted this to end, I wasn't just talking about last night. I meant all of this. You, me, and Adrien."

"And whatever other children may come along." Soren purrs into my ear, and his hot breath sends a chill down my spine.

"Oh, really?" I nip at his earlobe as he lifts me into his arms. "You're serious about this?"

"I've never been more serious in my life." He carries me down the hall into the bedroom, expertly shutting the door and locking it behind us.

My body tingles with excitement as we approach the bed. Last night was wild, but something tells me that tonight is going to be even better. Mostly because we're both fully in control of our faculties.

He dumps me onto the bed and pulls the borrowed, too-big pajama bottoms off me without missing a beat.

"Soren..."

He hovers over me with a hungry grin. "Just relax and let me pamper you." He kneels on the floor between my legs as they dangle off the edge of the bed.

My breath catches in my throat at the feeling of his lips on my cock. The heat of his mouth spreads across my body. His tongue slides along my dick, coaxing it to its full length. Feeling myself get hard while his lips and mouth surround me is a heady experience. It's not easy to keep my voice quiet, especially when every sensation threatens to cause another gasp or moan of pleasure.

I prop myself up on my elbows so I can see better.

Soren is intent on his work. His head bobs up and down in a slow, steady pace that feels heavenly on my sensitive skin. His eyes lift to meet my gaze but he never ceases showering my dick with lavish attention. Looking into his eyes fills me with a brand-new sensation, and I immediately understand that I truly am his omega.

I belong to him and him alone.

His love for me extends beyond any other relationship I've ever encountered.

We're inseparable now.

And I'm happier than I've ever been before.

Soren's not content to just suck me off, though. His hands are already working along my thighs, caressing the curves and inching steadily toward my asshole.

"Someone's excited," he says, pulling his head away from my cock to catch his breath. "You're already so slick down here."

To emphasize his point, he teases my hole with one of his fingers.

I gasp in response and let out a long, low moan. "It's not nice to tease me like that."

"I want to, though." He pauses to lick the precome from the head of my cock. "I want to learn every inch of your body. What makes you moan, what makes you shiver, what makes you come."

His curious finger slides a little farther into my opening, rubbing and exploring everything he can reach.

"Oh...fuck..." I gasp, in a whispered moan. "If you keep this up, I'm gonna come."

"Good." Soren ducks his head down again and captures my cock in his mouth. He slides his lips all the way to the base of my dick, taking me fully into his mouth. Meanwhile, he adds a second finger and begins to slowly fuck my asshole.

"Soren..." I gasp his name as I collapse back against the bed. My back arches as I thread my fingers through his hair.

Soren's mouth tightens around my cock and his head pumps up and down, matching pace with his fingers. He's not going to stop until I come. With the rate he's going now, he won't have to wait long.

"Oh...there...there!" My voice breaks for a moment as his fingers find the perfect spot. My mind goes blank, and the sensations rippling through me are unbelievable. My balls are painfully tight as the orgasm builds in the pit of my stomach. I'm so close that I can think of nothing else.

"Yes, yes, fuck, yes." My hands press Soren to take my cock deeper. Instinctively, I buck my hips and my balls spasm. Come rushes from me in a blinding fury.

In an instant, I'm spent. Gasping for breath, I release my hold on Soren and free him from my grasp. "I'm sorry." I pant for a moment to catch my breath as he rises from the floor. "I didn't mean to hold you down like that."

"Don't apologize." He waggles his eyebrows, licking his lips and standing over me. "I'm glad you enjoyed it that much."

I chuckle. "I don't think I've ever come that hard before."

A mischievous grin crosses his lips. "That wasn't even my best effort."

20

SOREN

I STEP out of the courthouse with a newfound happiness. The sun is shining, fluffy clouds drift across a brilliant blue sky, and birds sing from the treetops surrounding the parking lot.

Adrien and Luke are walking beside me, and the smiles on their faces reflect my own.

I pause on the sidewalk beneath the shade of a big tree and look at my family. "Where should we go to celebrate?"

Today, Luke formally adopted Adrien as his son. The three of us had already made a pact to be a family, but now, it's written in stone.

"Ice cream?" Adrien asks, looking up at me wistfully.

"That's exactly what I was thinking." I give Adrien a high-five. "What do you think, Luke?"

"You guys will have to enjoy it for me." He gives a slight grimace as he gingerly strokes the swell of his pregnant belly. "This little one will not forgive me if I eat dairy."

"Aww, baby. You gotta let Luke eat ice cream." Adrien puts a hand on Luke's tummy. "It's really good. You'll like it, I promise."

Luke's five months pregnant, and he's been struggling with some pretty intense food aversions. His sense of smell has gone through the roof too. The weirdest things can set him off and make him nauseous. For the first few months, the morning sickness was really bad, but thankfully that's mostly calmed down now. As long as he's careful about what he eats, that is.

"We'll make up for it once the baby is born," Luke tells Adrien. "You can teach her all about your favorite foods."

Adrien smiles and gently pats Luke's tummy again. "You hear that, baby? We're gonna eat ice cream when you're born."

"She might have to get a little bigger first," I remind him. "It takes a while for babies to start eating regular food."

"Oh..." Adrien looks thoughtful as he contemplates Luke's baby bump.

I hold out a hand to him. "Until then, you and I will have to eat all the ice cream ourselves, okay?"

"Chocolate?" Adrien takes my hand and falls into step beside me.

"Chocolate sounds good to me." I nod in agreement.

As we approach the car, I catch sight of Adrien's therapist leaving the courthouse. He nods hello to me before heading to his vehicle. His testimony contributed favorably to us being able to move forward in getting the adoption formalized.

I don't even like to think about the misery and emotional trauma my ex inflicted on Adrien. Abandoning him with me was bad enough, but the rest of it...

I shake my head and push those thoughts aside. I'm not going to let any of that ruin this otherwise perfect day. I've spent enough emotional energy fretting about that asshole over these last few months.

Today is a day to focus on what really matters.

My family.

"I still can't believe you sold your car." Luke chuckles as he stands beside me and stares at the minivan.

"Our family is growing." I shrug nonchalantly. It was a spur-of-the-moment thing, but after setting the court date last week, I realized that my "status symbol" of a car didn't really fit me anymore.

It no longer reflected the things I valued.

"Yeah, but a sedan or a station wagon could've worked too. You jumped straight into 'soccer dad' mode."

"Well..." I slide the side door open so Adrien can climb inside. "Adrien starts school next month. We've already talked about signing him up for sports. I guess 'if the shoe fits?'"

Luke chuckles and kisses my cheek. "You've changed so much from when we first met," he says, opening the front passenger door.

"You like it, though." I wink at him.

"Maybe?" Luke grins playfully before climbing into the van.

"You guys are being gross again," Adrien chimes in from his seat in the back. "Can we just get ice cream?"

"Yes, yes, sorry." I laugh and double-check his seat belt. Satisfied that he's safely buckled in, I close the door and take my place in the driver's seat.

Only a few minutes later, the three of us are sitting on the outdoor patio of a nearby ice cream parlor. The patio opens out into a beautiful park. The river rolls by lazily and flocks of ducks gather by the waterside. It's hard to believe we're in the heart of the city.

"Careful, Adrien. It's dripping." Luke hands Adrien a napkin.

Adrien's struggling to keep up with his ice cream cone as it begins to melt in the afternoon heat.

"You gotta lick it." I hold up my ice cream cone and demonstrate the most effective method of sweeping up messy drips. "You can't just eat the top. You have to lick the whole thing."

Adrien does his best to mimic me, but he's still struggling. The double cone might have been a teeny bit too big for him, but we're going all-out today.

Luke cringes as chocolate drips down Adrien's shirt. "Oh well, I guess you'll just have to take a bath when we get home."

"Can we feed the ducks?" Adrien gestures toward the flock that's waddling through the grass nearby. We've visited this park a few times now, and the ducks are definitely Adrien's favorite part.

"We'll have to bring them some crumbs another time. I don't think ducks like ice cream very much."

"After the baby is born, I wanna show her how to feed the ducks." Adrien licks his knuckles, making even more of a mess. "And how to use the swings and the slide."

"Absolutely." I love imagining my kids playing together. I can't wait. "She'll have to learn how to walk first, though."

"I'll show her. Walking's easy." Adrien jumps up from his chair and demonstrates how good he is at it.

When we first learned that Luke was pregnant, Adrien wasn't exactly thrilled with the idea. Over the past few months, he's really warmed up to the idea, though. Now, he constantly talks about all the things he's planning to do with his sister once she arrives.

"What do you think about Marie?" Luke muses as he looks up from his phone. The search for a baby name has been unending. Nothing sounds quite right.

"It's not a bad name," I say before pausing to work on my ice cream cone.

"I don't like it." Adrien frowns and shakes his head, flinging strings of chocolate as he does. "It's too...old."

Luke sets his phone aside. "Well, what name do you like?"

"Umm…" Adrien looks around for a minute and then his face lights up. "Duck."

"Duck?" Luke shakes his head and laughs. "You can't name your sister Duck."

"Why not?" Adrien cocks his head to the side and squints. "Ducks are cool."

"Yes, but your sister isn't a duck. She's a baby. She needs a human name." Luke smiles softly and rests his elbows on the table.

"Human names are dumb." Adrien pouts before returning to his ice cream.

Luke gives me a pleading look.

"Well, what about your name?" I ask. "Do you like your name?"

Adrien looks like I just asked him the strangest question in the world.

"Your name is a human name. Just like my name and Luke's name." I'm not sure he's following my logic here, but I can't think of a better way to explain it.

"I still like Duck the best."

"We'll keep that in mind." I keep my expression stoic and try to seem sincere. "If we can't find a better name, maybe we'll come back to it."

Adrien doesn't look thrilled with that suggestion but he doesn't fight it. "Okay."

"At this rate, we'll have to call her Jane Doe." Luke sits back in his seat and looks up at the sky. "I feel like we've been over every single possible name."

"We've still got plenty of time to figure it out." I'm not nearly as worried as he is. I know we'll find the perfect name for her. "There's no reason to rush. Something will come up."

"I didn't think it would be this hard," Luke says with a sigh. "I've got a dozen different boy names picked out, but I have no idea what to name a little girl."

I look out at the water and smile. "Well...if all else fails, Adrien's got a backup plan for us."

Luke frowns at me and rolls his eyes. "You better hope we find something else or she might end up being called Adriena."

21

SOREN

"Here, you can stir." I set the bowl of cookie dough on the table in front of Adrien. "Just don't eat any of it."

"Why not?" Adrien masterfully takes hold of the big mixing spoon I hand him.

"Because then there won't be any left for cookies." I can't help but smile as he does his best to stir the dough. It really doesn't need to be stirred anymore, but it gives him something to do and lets him feel like he's helping.

My grandma used to do the same thing when I was little.

While Adrien is hard at work, I clean up the mess of cookie ingredients that have spread across the kitchen counters. Things kind of got out of hand, but I wanted Adrien to be involved in the process as much as possible.

After all, there are only a few weeks left until he's no longer an only child.

I'm so pregnant, I can barely see the tips of my toes when I look down now. My feet ache, my back is killing me, and my cankles make it hard to wear socks. Right now, I really just want to go sit down, but I'm determined to finish these cookies.

One of my biggest fears is that Adrien will resent his sister when she gets here. He's excited about being a big brother right now, but once he realizes how demanding babies are, I'm worried he'll feel replaced.

That's why I'm doing my best to make time for him and let him know that he's loved.

Thankfully, with Soren working from home, we should be able to switch off baby duties and make sure Adrien still gets one-on-one time with each of us.

"This is hard work." Adrien pants exaggeratedly as he keeps working on the dough. "Making cookies is hard."

"Yeah, but it's gonna be worth it." I peek into the bowl to check on his progress. "You're doing great, and when we're done, you'll be able to share them with your friends at practice tonight."

Adrien's been having a blast learning how to play soccer with other kids his age. Their first game is next week, and he's super excited about the whole thing.

"Do you think the baby will like cookies?" Adrien asks after a moment.

"Well, she won't have any teeth when she's born, but I'm sure she'll love them when she does."

"Can we teach her how to make cookies too?" Adrien puts his spoon down and shakes out his arms like a powerlifter prepping to lift a heavy weight.

"Yeah, when she's a little older."

"Once she can walk?"

"Probably when she learns how to talk a bit." I put the last of the dirty dishes in the sink. "That's when my grandma started to teach me."

Adrien returns to stirring with renewed gusto. "I wanna make the best cookies just like your grandma, so I can teach the baby."

I smile as I return some of the ingredients to the refrigerator. The door of the fridge is a veritable art gallery now. A cascade of beautiful paintings flutter in the breeze as I close the door. I've been wanting to reduce the number of paintings on the door without discouraging our budding artist, but I haven't quite been able to yet.

It's definitely a work in progress.

Meanwhile, we're less than a month out from the baby's arrival and we still haven't come up with a name. Much to my chagrin, Soren's taken to calling her "Ducky" when Adrien's not around.

"I think it's all stirred up." Adrien stops stirring, which is code for him being bored with it.

"Okay, let me get the cookie sheet." I snap my thoughts back to the present and grab the cookie sheets from the counter where they're already waiting.

"We're gonna take these spoons." I hand Adrien a regular table spoon and then demonstrate the technique. "And we're gonna scoop up some dough and plop it on the sheet like this. Not too big, though," I say as he loads up his spoon. "If it's too big, they won't come out right."

Adrien carefully adjusts his cookie dough and mimics my motion to put it on the sheet. "Did you do this with your grandma?"

"All the time. She loved to make cookies." I smile softly at the memory. Every Saturday morning, my grandma would help me make a big batch of cookies, and we'd eat them with our lunch all week long. It was during those baking sessions that I learned a lot of important life lessons.

As I got older, our conversations matured as well. That was my time to open up and share all the troubles in my life. I could have gone to her at any time, but there was something about Saturday morning that felt...right.

Without my grandma's guidance, there's no doubt in my mind that I wouldn't be where I am today.

My only regret is that she's not here to see the family I've found. She would've loved to sit at the table with us right now, answering all of Adrien's questions as we make cookies. She was a fountain of wisdom.

"What's wrong?" Adrien stops and stares at me. "You look sad."

I blink a few times and force myself to smile. "I'm okay. I was just thinking about how much I miss my grandma. You would've liked her."

Adrien looks thoughtfully down at his tray of cookies. "Was she nice?"

"Yes, she was very nice. She loved chocolate chip cookies and working in her garden."

"Did she like ducks?"

I shake my head at the reference and try to remember. "I don't know, actually. She liked chickens, though. She had a bunch of chickens, and they all had names."

"What's a chicken?" Adrien looks at me curiously. "Is it like a duck?"

"Yeah, I guess it is. They're a little different, though. I'll have to show you a picture when we're done." I frown as I put the last few balls of cookie dough on the sheet. After growing up on my grandma's farm, it hadn't occurred to me that Adrien might not know what a chicken is.

Maybe it's just the pregnancy hormones, but I'm overcome with a case of homesickness that's worse than anything I've felt in a long time. My vision blurs as a few tears slide down my cheeks. Before I can bite them back, it's too late, and I'm sobbing like a crazy person.

Adrien hops down from his chair and runs off without a word. I'd ask him where he's going, but I already know. This isn't the first time I've randomly burst into tears since becoming pregnant. He's got standing orders on what to do in this situation.

Not even a minute later, Adrien returns with Soren. I hate interrupting him in the middle of his work day, and seeing him makes me cry even harder.

"It's okay, my love." Soren gingerly slides my chair away from the table and kneels in front of me. "Whatever's the matter, it'll all be okay."

"I'm sorry." I sniffle as I try to get my emotions under control. "You shouldn't have to drop everything to come deal with me."

"I'm just about done for the day anyway." Soren brushes a few hairs off my brow. "But even if I wasn't, I'd drop everything in a heartbeat to be by your side."

I choke back a sob and start mopping my eyes with my shirt sleeves. "I don't deserve you."

"Not true in the slightest." Soren takes my hands in his. "You're my omega, and I'm your alpha. We belong together."

"Now." He presses his forehead to mine. "Tell me what's troubling you, my love."

I take a deep breath and try to gather my thoughts. "We were talking about my grandma." I clear my throat and sniffle before continuing. "And I started thinking about how much I miss her and the farm where I grew up. These stupid pregnancy hormones just blew it all out of proportion." I choke out a sobbing laugh. "It sounds dumb now that I've said it out loud."

"Not dumb at all." Soren presses his lips to my temple. "It's not dumb to miss the people we love."

He sits back on his heels and looks over at the cookie sheets. "What needs to happen next with these? What can I do to help?"

"They...um...need to go in the oven now." I sit up and look around to make sure there's nothing I forgot. "I'm sorry for melting down."

"You have nothing to apologize for. Right, Adrien?"

Adrien has been sitting patiently by the cookie sheets this entire time. He nods in agreement. "I was just worried you'd cry on the cookies."

I chuckle at his honesty. "I think I managed to avoid them."

His innocent remark drives away the last of the tears lingering in my eyes.

Soren quickly sweeps the cookie sheets away and places them in the oven. With the timer ticking, he returns to my side. "Why don't we move into the living room? I'll massage your feet, and Adrien can try out his new video game." Soren holds out a hand and helps me to my feet while Adrien skips ahead to turn on his game.

"Adrien was asking about my grandma." I lean against Soren and linger in the kitchen. "And he asked what chickens were. It just got me thinking about the farm again."

"What about it?" Soren gently asks.

"Do you think...I mean..." My voice trails off, and I shake my head. "It's a stupid idea."

"Do you want to move to the country?"

"Or somewhere near it. Some place where we can have chickens and maybe some ducks." I chuckle. "Maybe a goat or two."

Soren smiles softly and pulls me into a warm hug.

I rest against his chest and listen to the sound of his heartbeat. "We'll need to find a new place soon anyway." He gently rocks me back and forth. "The baby will sleep in our room for a while, but that won't last forever. I really don't want to ask Adrien to share his room with her. I think it's important for them to have their own space."

"And you need space for your office." I tilt my head to look up at him. Right now, he's using a corner of our bedroom for work. It's functional but not ideal.

"I'd like to get a dog too." Soren raises an eyebrow to gauge my response.

"We don't even have a place yet, and it's already turning into a zoo."

Soren leads me to the sofa and sits at my feet. He's got the magic touch when it comes to foot rubs. As he starts working on my aching feet, the tension in my muscles literally melts away.

"I've got a few contacts in real estate." Soren glances at the TV to see what Adrien is playing. "I'll have them sniff around and see what comes up. I'm sure you'd rather not move until after the baby is born, though."

I wrinkle my nose at the thought. "With my luck, I'd go into labor in the middle of the whole moving process. But it'll be good to get an idea of what's out there."

Soren nods in agreement, but then after a moment, his expression shifts and he looks up at me thoughtfully.

I can tell he's pondering something profound. His brow always gets this little wrinkle in it when he comes up with something brilliant. "What's on your mind?"

"Well..." Soren takes a deep breath and sits up a little straighter. "I just had a thought but...it might make you cry, so I just want to prepare you."

"Oh, boy, this should be fun." I roll my eyes playfully. "I make no promises since I have zero control over my hormones right now. You know that."

Soren inhales deeply and rests his hands on my knees. "Well, our daughter still needs a name."

I raise an eyebrow. "Yes?"

"What about...Helen?"

My grandmother's name. Why had that not occurred to me before? My vision blurs at the thought of naming my daughter after the most important woman in my life. I can't think of anything better.

But words fail me as a fresh tide of tears pour down my cheeks.

22

SOREN

"THAT'S IT! RUN, ADRIEN, RUN!" I cheer at the top of my lungs as I bounce along the sideline of the peewee soccer match. A small crowd of screaming parents is gathered alongside me, all cheering excitedly for their children as they race up and down the field after the ball.

Luke's on his feet beside me, cheering just as hard but not bouncing quite as much. We're just a few days out from our due date now, so Helen could make her arrival at any time. I told him he could stay home, but Luke refused to miss Adrien's first game.

We're coming up to the end of it now.

Adrien's team has been doing well, and I'm already picturing a professional soccer career for my son. If he wants it, that is. Who am I kidding? Every time he does something new, I catch myself daydreaming about him at the top of the field. Painting, soccer, video games, board games, even stupid stuff like tying his own shoes gets me more excited than I can explain.

With a powerful kick, Adrien sends the ball rolling toward the goal. This isn't his first shot of the day, but the other three attempts were either missed or caught.

This time, his timing is perfect, and the ball flies past the kid protecting the goal, earning the final point of the match.

I'm beyond ecstatic.

As the kids file off the field, I drop to my knees and hold out my arms. Adrien darts toward me with excitement in his eyes. "Did you see, Dad!?" He squeals as I wrap him in a big hug. "Did you see the goal I made!?"

"I did!" I'm grinning so big I think my cheeks are gonna split. "It was such a good shot."

"I'm gonna keep practicing." Adrien scrambles out of my arms. "Next time, no one's gonna block me."

"Good plan. What do you think, Luke?" I glance back and see Luke grimacing as he stares off into the distance.

"Luke?" I spring to my feet, panic giving me speed that I didn't know I possessed.

"I'm okay..." Luke says, smoothing his features and exhaling slowly. "I think...it was a contraction."

I freeze, and my mind suddenly goes blank. Contraction? What does that mean? It's important, I know that. We've been talking about this. Contraction means...

"Is it time?" I gasp as the neurons in my brain finally make the connection.

"I don't know..." Luke winces and presses a hand to his belly. "Probably?"

"Okay, okay... We know what to do." I dart to the left a few feet and then stop short. "Right, parking lot is the other way."

I start walking but then stop again. By the time I turn back, Luke is shaking his head.

"Stop panicking," he says with an exasperated sigh. "Give me the car keys and help Adrien get his stuff together."

I clumsily fish the keys out of my pocket. "But, you...the baby—"

"We'll be fine." Luke takes the keys from my hand just as he has to stop and grunt against the pain. "As long as you don't take forever getting to the car, we should have time."

I'm starting to wish I'd read more of those baby books we bought. I'm suddenly very aware of how unprepared I am.

Luke shuffles toward the parking lot without so much as a backward glance. How can he be so calm right now?

"Dad?" Adrien takes my hand and gives it a tug.

Looking down at him gives me a sense of purpose. I can't completely freak out right now. My family needs me to hold on to my rational mind. "Looks like your sister has decided to come celebrate your first soccer game with us." I crouch down to his eye level. "Luke's gonna wait in the car while we get your stuff together. Do you know where you left your bag?"

"Over there I think." He points to the bench where he and his team had been positioned on the sideline.

"Let's go get it. We've got to hurry."

A few minutes later, we're loaded into the van and on our way to the hospital. Every instinct is telling me to step on the gas so I can get my omega to help as soon as possible. But I resist.

The safety of my family is paramount.

I just hope we don't get stuck in traffic, because I'm not prepared to deliver this baby myself.

Through some miracle, we manage to skate through the downtown intersections without getting caught in gridlock. By the time we pull into the hospital, Luke's been having contractions for about thirty minutes.

I honestly don't know if that's long or not. He keeps telling me they're just little ones and we've got plenty of time. How does he know that, though? What if he's mistaken?

Under any other circumstance, I thrive in a crisis. I'm the person other people go to for guidance when the chips are down, because I stay calm and keep my shit together. But that calm, cool demeanor comes from knowing exactly what to do.

I have resources, I have contacts, and I can take action to avert a crisis or help others get through one.

Right now, unfortunately, I have none of that.

I don't really remember everything that happened after we got out of the car, but somehow, we end up in the delivery ward of the hospital. Nurses fuss endlessly over Luke for a few minutes while I sit nearby with Adrien.

And then, suddenly, it's just the three of us again.

Luke chuckles when he looks over at me. "You look like you're gonna puke."

"I feel like I'm gonna puke." I smile even though I'm not actually kidding. "How are you so calm?"

"I dunno." Luke shrugs and shifts his weight. "I think it's just time, ya know? I feel kind of Zen about the whole thing. Plus, I'm on some amazing painkillers right now."

My adrenaline begins to subside. We're gonna be okay. We made it to the hospital in one piece, and the people here are professionals. Luke's in good hands. I can finally relax.

"You should call Arlo," Luke reminds me.

"Right." I nod and pull out my phone.

We don't want Adrien to be in here when it's go-time because it might be traumatizing for him. Thankfully, Arlo offered to come to the hospital and stay with him in the waiting room.

"I don't wanna go with Arlo." Adrien crosses his arms over his chest at Luke's bedside. "I wanna stay with you guys."

"You'll be here." Luke places his hand on Adrien's shoulder. "But when it's time for Helen to be born, there'll be a lot of people in here and we don't want you to get squished. So you and Arlo are gonna wait in the other room. But you can come right back once she's born, I promise."

Adrien looks upset but doesn't say anything.

"Arlo said he'll bring some games to play with you," Luke says.

By the time I'm off the phone with Arlo, Adrien has calmed down and is telling Luke all about the amazing shot he made at the end of the game.

That helps me focus on what's in store for me and Luke over the next few hours.

When I've watched babies born in the movies or on TV, it's always a very quick affair. There's a lot of screaming, sweating, and sometimes copious amounts of hot water being boiled. But then, the baby arrives and everyone is smiling. It's usually done in the space of about ten minutes. Very rarely does it take the entire length of a TV episode.

I can now safely say that is all fantasy.

We're well into our third hour at the hospital before things even start to heat up. The term "active labor" keeps getting thrown around by several of the nurses, so I take that as a promising development.

Arlo arrived a few hours ago and now escorts Adrien to the waiting room to play games.

I must look like a lost puppy because one of the nurses takes me by the hand and directs me over to a seat beside Luke. "Hold your omega tight." She places Luke's hand in mine. "He's going to need to borrow your strength now."

Her words snap me out of my haze, and I nod in understanding.

My gaze settles on Luke. My beautiful omega, the light of my life. "I love you," I tell him as I press a kiss to his forehead. "And I'm here."

"Nice of you to show up." Luke blows a long breath through his teeth. "Things are just starting to get interesting."

Hearing him make jokes eases the tension that's been weighing me down.

Everything's going to be okay.

EPILOGUE
LUKE

THE DUCKS QUACK EAGERLY, waddling across their yard as Adrien and I approach the fence.

"Here you go, ducks!" Adrien starts tossing vegetable scraps into the yard. "Come get your snack, ducks!"

Adrien's gone through a growth spurt over the last year. He's no longer the timid little five-year-old I met in Soren's apartment almost two years ago. We're approaching his seventh birthday, and I can barely believe it.

So much has changed that there are times when I wonder if it's all a dream.

"Do you think there are any eggs?" Adrien asks, looking up at me.

"Why don't you go look in their house?" I help him open the door to the pen so none of the ducks escape.

When we first started building our feathered flock, Adrien was a little timid around them. For all of his love of ducks, they're definitely a little overwhelming at first. But now, his confidence has grown, and he strides across their grassy yard without hesitation.

The duck house is a cute little shed that Soren built from a set of plans he found online. It was one of his first woodworking projects, so he's quite critical of it.

Personally, I think it's perfect and it does the job just fine.

Adrien goes inside the shed while I give the ducks the rest of their dinner.

We bought our little farm on the edge of town a few months after Helen was born. It's nothing fancy, just a few acres and a lovely farmhouse set back from the road.

Having a place for the ducks was a priority, of course. Eventually, I want to get some chickens, but that'll have to wait a bit. Right now, all our extra attention has gone toward the tree house that's slowly coming together in the backyard.

But we're not really in a hurry. Now that we've moved in, we can take all the time we need to make sure things are done right.

"I found one!" Adrien emerges from the duck house with an egg in one hand. He proudly carries it across the yard to me.

"Nice." I help him slip out of the pen without anyone escaping.

We've had a few incidents with escapees in the past, so we're doubly careful. In fact, there's still a duck or two that have gone and made a life for themselves down by the creek.

"Do you think the peaches are ripe yet?" Adrien asks, handing me the duck egg and looking up at me excitedly. The rate at which he switches topics is dizzying sometimes.

"It's still a bit early, but we can check." I fall into step behind him as he trots off to check the small orchard that came with the house. I doubt there's much change from when we were out there yesterday evening, but this has become a ritual of sorts.

Every evening, Adrien and I go out and feed the ducks, then walk in the orchard for a little bit. Eventually, there might be something to pick out there, but for now, it's an excuse to stretch our legs and enjoy the cool evening air.

As we walk beneath the branches of the peach trees, the sound of the screen door catches my attention. My gaze drifts toward the back porch where Soren is walking down the steps with Helen in his arms.

It feels like just yesterday that we brought her home from the hospital. Now...

Soren reaches the bottom of the steps and sets her on her feet in the soft grass.

She squeals excitedly and takes his hand when he offers it. Together, they walk toward the orchard to join me and Adrien.

"Helen!" Adrien kneels down in the grass and holds out his arms to his sister.

She eagerly lets go of Soren's hand and trots toward Adrien at the fastest speed she can manage with her short little legs.

"Good job!" Adrien praises her when she reaches him. "You're getting so good at running. Isn't she?"

"Absolutely." I run my fingers through her fine hair. "She's gonna be an Olympic sprinter for sure."

"She's certainly outpacing me," Soren says as he reaches my side. "I can barely keep up with her." He gives me a quick kiss in greeting and slides an arm around my shoulders.

"I don't know how you do it all day," Soren continues.

"When Adrien's home, I have him chase her." I chuckle. "But now that school's starting again, I'm gonna be getting a workout, for sure."

Adrien grins. "She's not super fast yet. You old people can still beat her."

"Hey, who are you calling old?" Soren protests playfully.

Helen babbles as if trying to join in the conversation.

"See? She agrees with me." Adrien holds up his hand to high-five her. It's a trick we've been trying to teach her.

"No, she's saying that you should respect your parents." Soren scoops Helen up in his arms and tickles her tummy.

"I bet she doesn't even know what that means." Adrien laughs and falls into step beside Soren. Together, they continue to walk through the orchard.

"I hate to break it to you, buddy, but she doesn't know what anything means."

I chuckle silently and follow the three of them. Moments like these will live forever in my memory.

"What are you doing all the way back there?" Soren stops and looks back at me.

"Just enjoying the view of my beautiful family." I jog to reach his side, a dreamy smile on my lips.

Helen leans toward me, her little arms outstretched. I sweep her into my arms with a little spin that makes her giggle. "You three are all I need to be truly happy. I could be living in a shoebox and only eating baked beans, and I'd be happy as long as I had you all."

"That's an oddly specific scene." Soren winks with a playful grin.

"I don't even like beans," Adrien adds.

"I'm trying to be sincere, you guys." I huff as they burst into laughter. I can't help but smile along with them. "I mean it, though."

"I know you do, my love." Soren gives me a kiss. "No matter where we go or what happens, we'll be okay as long as we have each other."

"Just no beans..." Adrien adds.

"You liked the chili I made the other night, and it had beans in it." I peek around Helen's chubby hand that she's waving in my face.

"Chili is different. We had hot dogs with it."

"Hot dogs make everything taste good," Soren agrees with a solemn nod.

I honestly can't tell if they're serious or just playing around. "What about all those green beans you ate out of the garden?"

"Those...aren't real beans?" Adrien shrugs. "I don't know. Dad, you wanna race?"

He's obviously eager to end the conversation and escape further scrutiny over his eating habits.

That's when I resolve to slip beans into every meal for the rest of the year.

Or at the very least, until the end of summer.

"On your mark." Soren begins the countdown for their race, and Adrien eagerly takes a runner's stance. Track has become his latest obsession after watching the Summer Olympics recently.

"Get set."

"Go!" Adrien's off like a shot, sprinting along the path that loops around the outside of the orchard. Soren lopes along after him, not really expending much effort to keep up. Maybe once Adrien gets a little older, he'll start to race him for real. For now, he stays just close enough that it encourages Adrien to push himself to go faster.

They disappear from sight as the path curves around the trees.

I smile to myself and keep walking with Helen in my arms. She's content to look at everything around us, chattering happily. Birds singing in the trees nearby catch her attention for a few seconds before she starts babbling again.

For my part, I'm happy to ask her questions and encourage her to continue talking. She's not much of a conversationalist, but she'll get there eventually. Adrien already swears he can understand her.

A few minutes pass before I hear Soren and Adrien laughing and shouting at each other behind me. I scoot over to the side of the path and hold out one arm as a makeshift finish line when they gallop toward me in a cloud of dust.

Soren pulls up just shy, letting Adrien reach my arm first so he can tap it for the win.

Red-faced and sweaty, panting with effort, Adrien turns to face Soren. "Hey, you let me win!"

"I did not. I tripped on a root." Soren points to a nearby root that certainly looks like it could be the guilty party.

"Race me again, for real this time," Adrien demands, not buying the root theory for a minute.

"I think it's time to head inside and get cleaned up," I intervene, nipping their rivalry in the bud. "Adrien, you promised you'd take a bath tonight. Remember?"

"Yeah, just one more race?" Adrien hops up and down like a racer trying to get his muscles warmed up.

"It's getting dark already." I gesture to the sky overhead. "If you want dessert tonight, then we should head inside."

Adrien pouts but doesn't protest.

"Tomorrow night," Soren says with a nod. "We'll have a rematch, okay?"

"And this time, you gotta race me for real." Adrien waves goodbye before sprinting toward the house.

"I'm more out of shape than I thought," Soren says, gasping for breath beside me as we walk to the back door. "It's not going to be long before he's actually beating me."

"I guess that means you need to get moving, old man," I tease.

"I might be old, but I've still got plenty of stamina." Soren shoots me a mischievous wink.

"Soren!" I nod toward Helen who is chattering happily in his arms.

"What?" He gives me an innocent shrug. "I didn't say anything!"

After a quick kiss, he jogs off after Adrien, leaving me laughing to myself.

It might have taken a long, roundabout path to get here, but I finally know what it means to be on top of the world.

<u>**Order Now**</u>